I0608534

The Joyous, Consequential Life
of Dr. Francisco Marquez

Ryan Starrett

En Route Books and Media, LLC
Saint Louis, MO

⊕ *ENROUTE*

Make the time

En Route Books and Media, LLC

5705 Rhodes Avenue

St. Louis, MO 63109

Contact us at

contactus@enroutebooksandmedia.com

Cover Credit: Sebastian Mahfood

Copyright 2025 Ryan Starrett

ISBN-13: 979-8-88870-362-5

Library of Congress Control Number: 2025937075

All rights reserved. No part of this book may be reproduced, stored in a retrieval system, or transmitted in any form, or by any means, electronic, mechanical, photocopying, or otherwise, without the prior written permission of the author.

Chapter 1

He turned sideways as he reached the door leading into the school. He squeezed his immense bulk through and slowly waddled to his new office. He took one look at the chair in front of his new desk and realized the school had not been prepared for his rotundity.

With a huge sigh, he plopped down into the chair. It groaned and shifted beneath his weight. First order of business: invest in a new, double-wide, steel-reinforced chair. He raised his arms and put them behind his head and folded his hands and gazed out his window at the community he intended to win over to his *weltanschauung*. He had fled a university professorship, an elected political office, and a successful corporate job. Now, he found himself the principal of a small Catholic high school with an enrollment of eighty-one students and little prospect for more.

The school was located near the end of the world—or the center, according to who was queried. It stood on a small rise on the outskirts of the seemingly never-ending Mississippi Delta. Luckily for his health, the nearest fast-food chain was fifty miles away, roundtrip. Unluckily for his health, it was a German community that lived on steak, starch, and white gravy. Three such restaurants stood within four walking blocks of his new house. Two more eateries that specialized in fried crispitos, fried chicken, fried jalapenos, fried cheese, and fried pies were also in the vicinity.

The town was governed by the triune deity of football, beer, and Catholicism—in that order. Five plus months a year, this holy trinity manifested itself in the outdoor cathedral flanked by two golden field goal posts and two sets of bleachers. A silver wafer was tossed in the air to signify the start of the service. Beer in plastic containers was passed discreetly from hand to hand and, after a while, not so discreetly. Meanwhile choirs of spectator-participants in their ziggurat pews offered a variety of prayers and supplications to God Almighty and his hierarchy of angels and saints. Saints Christopher, Michael, Sebastian, among others, were consistently invoked to come to the aid of the hometown team. In particularly pivotal moments, the intercession of Mary herself was requested. Win or lose, the service always concluded with a procession to the local bar where another *koinonia* commenced.

Politically, the town stood somewhere between Rush Limbaugh and Ann Coulter Republicanism. In recent years, the Democrats had made some inroads, bringing their membership up to four, which in turn increased the vigilance and anxiety of the other one thousand five hundred and forty-eight citizens, and a borderline fascist backlash was imminent. So great was the fear that these Democrats were nightly plotting to establish the town's first abortion clinic, mosque, and gun-free school zone that a number of leading citizens began to discuss the legalities of secession from the state of Mississippi, and then annexation by the Vatican. For after all, they concluded, it is better to be ruled by a strong, conservative, authoritarian Pope than to live amongst Democrats. However, when it was soon pointed out that the current Pope was a proponent of pluralism and immigrant rights, the movement was put on hold until the Holy Spirit placed upon the throne of Peter a more worthy Vicar of Christ who would not cater to wetbacks.

It was in such a town that the new principal, Dr. Francisco Marquez, PhD, now sat in his office gazing out the window. He picked up the local paper he had bought that morning and crossed his ankles remembering fondly and sadly the days when he could cross his legs. Capable of reading sixteen hundred words a minute, a skill he had refined in many years of graduate school, he quickly digested the front page and its lead story detailing the minutes of the local 4-H Club meeting. He then proceeded to the forecast for the upcoming week and its effects on the local farmers and the two-a-day football practices now in progress. Page two contained two more stories about the upcoming football season, including an interview with the head coach and a half-dozen of his players. It was on page three that a letter to the editor caused the first of thousands of the booming, infectious, joyous laughs that would fill his office and the school throughout the next year. It read:

It has been brought to my attention that our local Catholic school is having its seniors read excerpts from Shakespeare's *Macbeth* and *Genesis*. I must express my disappointment in the school's choice of reading material as both stories contain an unhealthy amount of #$&ual references. Having our children read such filth can only be detrimental to their moral development. In any given situation, I often ask myself, "What would Jesus do?" Well, I happen to know that Jesus never would approve young men and women reading the pornography that is *Macbeth* and *Genesis*.

I am also increasingly alarmed at the number of pregnant women walking through our local grocery store. These monsters of fertility are a moral outrage. I am astonished at their audacity in announcing to the entire community that they have had #@$ in the all too recent past. What are we supposed to tell our young children when they ask why Mrs. So-and-So is suddenly so fat?

If all of us God-fearing mothers of Wilhelmsburg started to take their religion seriously, we would be able to keep such banalities from the minds of our innocent children. I, for one, am proud of the fact that I've taught my children every time they *think* about $%#, they run the risk of contracting a disease, dying, or causing the death of a puppy. My children, although they attend our increasingly heathen Catholic high school, still remain entirely uncontaminated by the @#$ual culture that surrounds them. By keeping them away from all @#$ual references and innuendos, I am certain that when they go off to college, they will have the moral fortitude to easily resist the temptations of the sweetest of sirens.

We are all aware that the greatest temptation to our young people today is #$%. Thus, I am very disappointed in our teachers for introducing such filth to our children and in those loose women who flaunt their all-too-recent @#$ual goings-on. I urge the good citizens of Wilhelmsburg to band together and drive these heathen teachers from our school and these sluttish women from our grocery store!

Signed,
A Very Concerned and Holy Catholic

Dr. Marquez wondered what kind of wonderfully absurd community he had been given the keys to. He did what he normally did when confronted with the hilarious absurdity of life—he laughed and reflected. He stored these life anecdotes in his mind and pondered them in his heart.

Chapter 2

Dr. Marquez sat across from his first hire, Mr. Ferro, the new Geography/Government/Economics/Mississippi History/8th Grade Science/ACT Prep/Golf coach from Macon, Georgia, at Schmidt's, one of the three local restaurants specializing in German cooking. The introduction and conversation had gone well. He was all-in-all pleased with his first hire. Mr. Ferro seemed intelligent, certainly motivated, and sufficiently human. The semi-well-endowed waitress brought them complimentary biscuits. He had noticed her endowment from the corner of his eye. Mr. Ferro had noticed, too, but not from the corner of his eye. Dr. Marquez noticed the signs of desperate infatuation. Mr. Ferro's heart was racing, he talked nervously, and he was easily distracted.

A semi-productive conversation ensued with the semi-well-endowed waitress making periodic inquiries into the meal, service, and potentiality for dessert. Mr. Ferro's eyes made what Mr. Ferro thought were discreet glances at the waitress's chest. Gradually, he came to focus on her face, particularly her eyes, and then his own eyes began to dance. Seeing into Mr.

Ferro's soul, Dr. Marquez thought: "I wonder who he'll fall in love with next?"

Chapter 3

Later that afternoon, Dr. Marquez met with his inherited Spanish teacher, Ms. Nina Yerma. She was as petite as he was large and as lithe and quick on her feet as he was plodding and methodical. Nevertheless, Dr. Marquez recognized a kindred spirit. Ms. Yerma and Dr. Marquez shared an unquenchable passion for education and indefatigable enthusiasm. He knew he was going to get along fine with this tiny temple of energy.

As soon as he finished outlining his expectations and vision for the Spanish department, Dr. Marquez noticed Mr. Ferro walking by the office on his way to his classroom. Since the meeting was just about to be adjourned, he suggested introducing Ms. Yerma, the veteran teacher of one year, to his new hire. The two walked down the hall toward Mr. Ferro's room, he ponderously, she restrained, forcing her hamstrings and calves to walk at, to her, an intolerably pedestrian pace.

They finally made their way to Mr. Ferro's room, knocked, and entered. The new teacher's eyes acknowledged his principal and then lit up at the sight of Ms. Yerma. Looking straight into her large brown eyes, but at the same time noticing the body of the vixen before him, Mr. Ferro awkwardly extended his right hand to make a proper introduction. Her tanned hand contrasted with his pale one; her long, thick, jet-black hair with his receding hairline; and her confidence with his timidity. Dr. Marquez was confirmed in his initial suspicions: Mr. Ferro was in love again.

Chapter 4

The first day had been productive. Dr. Marquez had met two of his colleagues, given an interview to the local paper, made a dozen or so calls to parents, and began to organize his new office. Now, he sat on his back porch with a glass of Bacardi 151 and a Romeo y Juliet cigar. He began to reflect again on the path that had brought him so far from the Florida Keys, the land of his birth; so far from Puerto Rico where he had taught at the University; so far from Los Angeles where he held an elected public office.

Being a principal of a small, downward-spiraling Catholic school, deeply in debt and with a shrinking enrollment, was the last place he thought he would be ten years ago. But here he was, and here he intended to thrive.

After he had been chosen principal and given the proverbial—and literal—keys to the school, he had returned home. He had told Fr. Pat that he felt he was supposed to be here in Wilhelmsburg, but as he drove home, he began to wonder if this was, after all, true. The Board had hired him after only a day of deliberation. Evidently, they too felt he was called to be there. He had accepted the position, but the car ride home had been a real challenge. Had he made the right decision? What was he committing to? Was it even possible to turn *this* school into a success?

The first half hour, he lamented the lack of good restaurants. How would he survive off the heavy German food so alien to his constitution? He had perused the local grocery and left unimpressed—no lobster, generic black beans, crumbling tortillas, and Vietnamese farm-raised tilapia. The quality of food alone was temptation enough to call the Board and tell them that he had reconsidered and would seek employment elsewhere, likely Florida, the Gulf Coast, or some other seaside community.

After much deliberation, he resolved to endure the culinary shortcomings of Wilhelmsburg, but then another thought assailed him. He could simply call the Board, refuse the position, and hit the open road, trusting that he would find something more amenable to his tastes. During the last several years, his relationship with God had deepened and he had placed more and more trust in His grand plan. Trust had led him to Wilhelmsburg. He had gotten hired after one interview. He had a steady income and prospects. But what if he cast the die again? What if he leapt into the wind and trusted that he would land at an even more advantageous position? Turn down security and place all his trust in God? Surely, he'd be rewarded. As nervous as he was to settle in Wilhelmsburg, as tempting as blind trust and surrender appeared, Dr. Marquez mentally recommitted himself to Holy Family and turned his focus to the detailed minutiae of a cross-country move.

His mind began to pack and distribute his accumulated possessions as he drove further and further from his new home and nearer his old, familiar lodgings. As he mentally gave away the possessions that wouldn't fit into a U-Haul, he realized how much he had actually accumulated, and how many connections, and powerful ones at that, he had made. Why was he settling for a position as a small-town, Catholic school principal? Surely, he was destined for greater things. He was only forty-five, connected, and relatively healthy. He had the world at his fingertips, and all he need do was reach out a little and close his hand upon it. Wealth, fame, power could all be his in just another five years in the real world. Why settle? Wilhelmsburg versus the World. Why toil and suffer in Wilhelmsburg when he could rule Stanford, Miami, or Google?

"No! No! No!" he told his wandering mind. "Holy Family and Wilhelmsburg are my focus now. They're my commitment. They'll get the fruits of my labor. Life goes on, and so has mine."

Chapter 5

"Are you fucking blind?!?! Do you even know what 'holding' is? That sonovabitch had *three* handfuls of jersey!"

Hoss Schilling glared at the referee as he unleashed another barrage from his repertoire of profanities. He had one of Wilhelmsburg's smallest and most colorful vocabularies. Visiting referees had heard it all before, but never quite in the same order and syntax as Hoss gave it to them. At two hundred and sixty pounds, most in the biceps, a little in the gut, Hoss was rarely told to can it.

It was the first game of the year, and with each missed call and each sip from his Styrofoam cup, Hoss' insults grew more and more colorful. Dr. Marquez had listened to the same six or seven words arranged, maneuvered, bastardized, and re-arranged for half the first quarter. This would be his first test of authority. He made his way to the fence where Hoss was giving the side judge three earfuls between draughts.

"It's Hoss, isn't it?" he said, extending his hand.

Hoss took the hand, keeping his eyes on the side judge. "Those glasses need to be strengthened you son of an asshole bitch!"

Turning finally to Dr. Marquez, he asked, "Can you believe this crew tonight? Unbefuckinglievable!"

"Yeah, they sure seem one-sided. And it's not our side. I'd like to believe this is their last game."

"No shit, Doc."

"But Hoss, don't you think you're laying it on a bit thick? I mean there's kids running around all over the place. Hell, Hoss, there's mechanics sitting up in the stands getting squeamish at your choice of words."

Hoss let out either a laugh or a grunt, that morphed into a scowl when Dr. Marquez inquired about the contents of his cup.

"Now, Hoss, you know the Mississippi High School Athletics Association doesn't allow alcohol to be consumed during games."

"Fuck them! These refs they gave us make a man drink. It's no wonder I'm not injecting this shit straight into my veins the way these cunts are screwing us."

"Hoss."

"Fuck you too! I ain't one of your students, Doc."

"C'mon, Hoss. You're a big guy, the biggest I've seen yet in Wilhelmsburg. But I'm not too shabby myself. I'm probably the only guy within a hundred miles with arms bigger than you."

Hoss finally turned to face the town's newest resident: "Just what are you sayin', Doc?"

"Now Hoss, I'm not going to fight you. I'm a Christian man and I've foresworn violence. But I am going to use these two arms and give you the biggest bear hug you ever received. From one Christian to another."

For the first time in years, Hoss Schilling had nothing to say. He stood there, mouth agape, staring at the smiling behemoth before him. Half a minute passed before Dr. Marquez said: "How about you drop that cup off in your car, Hoss? You do that, and I'll tell you what I'll do. Steve Knabe is a friend of mine, and he brought me some fresh venison just this morning. Tomorrow night, you and me will cook up that backstrap and down as much whiskey as you care to. Well, you'll take care of the whiskey; I'll stick to my rum. Bacardi 151, that's my drink of choice. I'll light up my cigar and we can discuss these shitty refs without all these kids around."

Eventually these words sank into Hoss' mind, and he dutifully walked to his car. When he came back, he still had his Styrofoam cup, but the sweet, smoky smell had been replaced with a neutral one. Ms. Yerma, the cheerleading coach, who had stood between Hoss and the refs all night long, stole a glance at the cup and was the first to see the water. "It's a miracle," she thought, "Dr. Marquez turned Hoss' whisky into water."

Chapter 6

Dr. Marquez was curious to see how his second hire, Mr. Meyer, Bachelor of Fine Arts, would fit in at Holy Family. Five weeks into the semester, he had to admit, satisfactorily. He had an easy-going, semi-hip/cool/contemporary personality, and, more importantly, an easy grading system, but most importantly, an impressive resume. Mr. Meyer had spent the last nine years teaching at Cedar Hill Public School. Now Dr. Marquez could introduce him to prospective students and parents as a veteran teacher with ten years (after the current year) teaching experience.

A precursory search into Mr. Meyer's B.F.A. background revealed that he had, indeed, been awarded a B.F.A.—after seven years in college. Dr. Marquez, able to put a positive spin on any situation, told his donors that Mr. Meyer had been an *uber*-Senior—two steps above a super-senior. This had been quite an effective promotion in the German community. Not only had Dr. Marquez appealed to German pride, but B.F.A. contained the exact same number of letters as Ph.D., and all the former letters were capitalized. All future hires with a mere MA would be at an automatic disadvantage. Dr. Marquez intended to rectify this misunderstanding in the future, but not yet. The B.F.A. v. PhD v. MA discrepancy might lead to an additional enrollee or two in the upcoming school year.

Chapter 7

Dr. Marquez waddled into the cafeteria. Mr. Ferro and Mr. Meyer were seated with the Wednesday meal, "mystery-on-a-stick," before them. Dr. Marquez rarely came to the cafeteria on "Cooks' Choice Wednesday," but as an aficionado of life he could not always stifle his curiosity.

He saw and heard exactly what he had expected. Mr. Ferro was making repeated, passing glances at Ms. Yerma's derriere, and Mr. Meyer was talking about the Wednesday menu at Cedar Hill nine years ago, the first year that he was voted "Faculty Favorite," just a year after he received his B.F.A. degree.

Ms. Yerma received her tray, turned one hundred and eighty-degrees and made her way to the faculty table. Simultaneously, Mr. Ferro adverted his eyes and stared at the mystery meat impaled on the stick before him, just in time to catch the end of Mr. Meyer's soliloquy: "...at Cedar Hill was tolerable. What I want to know is how it is that the federal regulations got stricter but the food worse?"

Dr. Marquez waited until the last student received his tray and then got his own three mysteries on a stick. He rejoined his faculty and relished every bit of that lunch time conversation: Mr. Meyer's reminisces of his own greatness at Cedar Hill, Mr. Ferro's attempted discreet glances at Ms. Yerma, and Ms. Yerma's quizzical looks at the others' trays of food as she picked delicately and discernibly at her plate of vegetables. Dr. Marquez loved people, especially characters, and he had plenty of characters on his staff. He resolved to eat in the cafeteria as often as his schedule allowed.

Chapter 8

Dr. Marquez had been receiving visitors all day. He always kept his office door open, and when he wasn't teaching his own three classes, or running chess club, or directing traffic, or setting up for Mass, or leading retreats, or a score of other tedious, but necessary duties, he was talking to anyone and everyone who wished to stop by and chat. The crowds at his door seemed to only grow with each passing month.

On this particular day, two parents made their way in with their daughter. She had been enrolled at Holy Family since kindergarten, but now as a sophomore she was having difficulty in Mr. Meyer's class.

As soon as they entered, Dr. Marquez recalled an e-mail he had received late last night that he had intended to respond to sometime today, when the crowds diminished. He very quickly racked his steel trap of a mind and recalled the gist of the e-mail: "…VERY disappointed!... thinking about IMMEDI-ATELY withdrawing!!.... TERRIBLE, TERRIBLE teacher!... our daughter is PARALYZED with fear!... demand IMMEDIATE action!!!...FIRE HIM!!!" Dr.

Marquez knew anyone who wrote in all caps must be taken either very seriously or not seriously at all.

The Hoffmans were serious. And seriously funny, at least to Dr. Marquez. To others, the husband was intimidating, and the wife was hysterical—and intimidating on account of her husband. The daughter, curiously, was reserved and timid. Or perhaps, Dr. Marquez mused, her timidity was a natural consequence of such loud and aggressive parents.

Dr. Marquez struck peremptorily: "Now, Floyd, there's just not enough room in this office for you to come in bowed up like that. Between your brawn and my blubber, you'll leave no room for your wife and daughter."

All three of the Hoffmans froze and looked at Dr. Marquez quizzically. With the tension somewhat diffused, Dr. Marquez got straight down to business, an unusual practice for him as he enjoyed nothing more than casual banter.

"Lisa, I noticed your grades in English and spoke with Mr. Meyer. He thinks you're very bright but could use some extra help until you catch the hang of his class. Your other classes look just fine, so it must be a matter of Mr. Meyer's style. Now, Mr. Meyer is a fine, fine teacher with plenty of experience and a B.F.A. from one of our best universities. Sometimes we come across a subject we either don't like or struggle with. You see all those diplomas hanging on my office wall? I was a straight 'A' student, *summa cum laude*, in science, math, literature, history, but I'll tell you now, just between you and me, I never could get the hang of Greek. You know, all those strange conjugations." She didn't know, but she stared at his smiling face and nodded. "Yep, some people just need extra work in certain subjects. I bet that's all you need." She doubted, but continued to stare at the happy face, nodding. "We'll see if we can't get that English grade up there where your others are. How about working after school on Tuesdays and Thursdays with Mr. Meyer? Maybe he can explain it better to you when he doesn't have a class full of other students." She had ceased listening but continued to look glossy-eyed into the face that was no longer in focus, still nodding. "Good then that's settled."

He turned from the blank and still bobbing face and told Lisa's parents, without missing a beat: "And if that doesn't work out, she can come to my office each eighth period and I'll tutor her. No matter what, we're not going to let your daughter fail. Holy Family is not in the business of failing students. A little effort, and a little help and we'll have Lisa all caught up."

The Hoffmans, who had entered as wolves, left as sheep. Even Lisa, who had absentmindedly nodded her way through the latter half of the meeting, left in a better mood, no longer paralyzed by her fear of failure. She picked up her backpack and followed her parents out the office door.

Chapter 9

It was 5:07, thirty-seven minutes since the weekly faculty meeting was supposed to have ended.

Dr. Marquez was cheerful, as was his custom. The teachers were arguing, as was theirs.

Meyer: "At Cedar Hill we had a teacher stand at the front door as the students entered school, and if they weren't wearing the proper shoes, they were sent home. Seems simple to me."

Babs Horvath (inherited Math teacher): "But what is a 'proper shoe?' I mean, are we supposed to look for brand names on the shoe? What about checking for a non-marking soul? How are we supposed to do that?"

Coach Koch: "What type of boots are acceptable shoes?"

Meyer: "A boot's a boot and a shoe's a shoe. Let's just call it what it is."

Horvath: "So we are or we're not allowing boots if they otherwise meet the dress code?"

Samantha Briton (the other inherited Math teacher, devoted to the Handbook): "I looked at the dress code in the teacher's handbook before this meeting, and it says the students must be wearing 'black, leather shoes with no logos.'"

Horvath: "Yes, but is a *boot* a *shoe*?"

Meyer: "A boot's a boot and a shoe's a shoe. At least that's how we defined it at Cedar Hill the ten years I taught there."

Koch: "Why can't a black, leather boot with no logos be a shoe?"

Briton: "I think if the Handbook wanted to allow boots, it would have said 'black, leather shoes or boots with no logos.' I think we should go by the Handbook."

Amusement to the contrary, Dr. Marquez decided it was time to intervene. He interjected: "Now that's an interesting question posed by Mrs. Horvath: is a boot a shoe? First, we must define our terms. What, exactly, is a shoe? What gives it its *quiddity*? In other words, what is the *form* of the shoe? And, when does it cease to be a shoe? Can a boot be a *species* of the *genre* 'shoe'?"

Dr. Marquez was met with quizzical, somewhat pained glances. Perhaps, he thought, I should not have made light of this topic. The teachers were, in fact, hurt, and he asked that they proceed and solve the riddle of the shoe.

Mr. Ferro would have been amused at Dr. Marquez's intervention, but his mind was on more serious matters. While the faculty debated the "whatness" of a shoe, he debated who he ought to take dancing and then home with him to his expensive hotel room. He had already decided the faculty meeting was a good time for a fantasy. This time, it would be at the Drury Inn in New Orleans. He and his date would go dancing, have a drink, and then go up to his spacious room with a large king-sized bed. But who to take? Ms. Yerma or Ms. Briton? In order for his fantasy to work, he needed to choose one or the other. Thus, as the teachers argued over shoes, he would turn his head in the direction of the speaker and steal glances at his potential fantasies.

Both had their merits. Ms. Yerma was so damn cute and petite—someone he could protect. Ms. Briton smiled at him every day with her mouth and eyes. And she had by far the better chest. Mr. Ferro seemed unusually engaged in the shoe-boot debate. But as his head swiveled from speaker to speaker, his mind was contrasting the attributes of one teacher versus another: eyes (Yerma), hair (Yerma), stomach (Yerma), smile (Briton), complexion (Yerma), breasts (Briton), derrière (undecided.)

Thus, an eternity unfolded as the pros and cons of two equally deserving vixens were exhausted.

Mr. Ferro had finally decided to roll the die and go with Ms. Briton. He felt good. Tonight, he would have an easy time falling asleep as his fantasy was already pre-arranged and awaiting him at home. Now, he turned his attention to the civil war raging all around him.

No longer was it a quasi-civil debate with each teacher making their points and politely second-guessing their opponents. Rather, it had evolved into a free-for-all reminiscent of an 1860-style congressional debate intermixed with Clay versus Adams versus Jackson rhetorical venom. Whichever side wound up on top, boot as shoe or boot as contraband, would see their *ex cathedra* pronouncement memorialized in the Handbook. And that was a prize worth fighting for.

Meanwhile, Dr. Marquez followed the controversy with evident interest. His demeanor was one of intense concentration as he gave all his attention to each speaker in turn. His innermost being, however, was thoroughly enjoying the absurdity of the situation. He was working hard to keep his guffaws on the inside.

The cacophony of insults reached its crescendo, and Dr. Marquez, fearing a chair being hurled or a walking cane being brandished, finally intervened and called a cessation to hostilities.

"I see both sides are amply acquainted with the matter at hand, and both sides are prepared to make this issue their Thermopylae. I suggest we establish a Dress Code Committee that will further investigate the pros and cons of allowing boots into our school. Any teachers who wish to contribute may e-mail me, and I'll work on setting up a four-member committee who will report their findings to the Parent Advisory Handbook Committee. If said committee is as equally divided as our faculty, then I'll present the findings to the Alumni Relations Improvement Committee. And if they, too, are unable to reach a decision, I'll form a six-person Council for the Appropriate Dressing of the Lower Leg Advisory Board, who will pass their decision on to the Bishop for approval."

This time Dr. Marquez's intervention was met with wide approval. Only Ms. Briton hesitated as she believed the wording of the CADLLAB unfairly biased the Board. "By calling the foot 'the lower leg,' don't you think it predisposes the Board to assume a boot is okay. Shouldn't it be called the Council for the Appropriate Dressing of the Foot Advisory Board?"

Dr. Marquez immediately said he would take the name into consideration and adjourned the meeting, just as half a dozen hands shot into the air in protest.

Chapter 10

Two hours after the decision to postpone the shoe-boot decision, another storm was brewing, this time at the Alumni and Supporters meeting. Per diocesan policy, the school was allowed only one fundraiser per year. Therefore, it was important to pick the right fundraiser.

This year, the frontrunner was "Chicken Shit Bingo." The concept was simple: set up a bingo board (53' by 53') on the football field; divide it into five columns and five rows (10'6" by 10'6"); fence in the 2,809 square foot area with barbed wire; have a local farmer donate a dozen chickens; feed them; let them shit at random; those who own the pre-bought card with five consecutive shatted upon numbers, win.

The fundraiser was estimated to bring in anywhere from $7,000 to $12,000. The controversy came over the naming of the event. Although the Alumni and Supporters committee was certainly not in the hands of the holy rollers, said rollers did have a vocal minority presence. And it was they who questioned the catholic-ness of a fundraiser that would condone the use of profanity. The rest of the board, who planned to settle the issue as quickly as possible and then adjourn to the local bar for their traditional Wednesday "six drinks at six" post-meeting wrap-up, were not pleased at having to sell the idea of their fundraiser. The idea of the "six at six" club was to begin promptly at six, finish all drinks and be home by eight. To begin at 6:30 would mean either sacrificing a drink or make getting home more of an adventure. A debate was the last thing they expected or wanted.

It seemed as if the holy rollers' objection would be mollified if the word "shit" were removed from the promotional material. But, what then could the fundraiser be called? Several suggestions were tossed around: "Chicken Crap Bingo?" "Chicken Feces Bingo?" "Chicken Fecal Matter Bingo?" "Chicken Dump Bingo?" "Chicken Excrement Bingo?" "Chicken Unplugged Bowel Bingo?" None of these suggestions seemed right. When one of the holy rollers suggested that the chickens not defecate at all but walk up to a square and turn around three times to mark the proper number, the other holy rollers began questioning the morality of having chickens deposit their turds in public in the first place. Surely, it would not be very Catholic to attend an event in which spectators watched unholy filth pour from the backside of any living being.

The more traditional Committee members immediately decided to squash the debate and go back to "Chicken Shit Bingo." However, the holy rollers had found a new crusade, and the proverbial shit hit the fan.

The holy rollers were concerned that throngs of people cheering defecating chickens would bring back too many memories of the ancient gladiatorial games in which so many Christians lost their lives. The innocent chickens would run around on a field as hundreds of Wilhelmsburg's citizens would hoarsen their throats screaming, "Shit! Shit! Shit!" And when the droppings hit the ground, exalted cheers and raised thumbs would reach into the air from those who possessed the shatted upon number. Such debauchery and licentiousness were not worthy of a Catholic school.

It was now 6:32 and the old guard of the Alumni and Supporters Committee had heard enough from the holy rollers, and profanities more profane than "shit" began to be bandied about, and not always from the same side.

Dr. Marquez had spent the last hour alone, quietly sitting in his office reflecting. The storm in the library grew more and more dangerous, but still he sat in bemused reflection. Finally, he arose and waddled toward the eye of the storm. He intended to pass by the library when one of the Committee members hailed him from a distance. He changed course and entered the maelstrom which did not abate with his presence while epithets involving fascism and threats of excommunication were hurled from one side to the other, yet all eyes did look to him. Immediately, he began to chuckle, louder and louder. Confused, both parties ceased their clamor, and silence rained down upon the library minus the chuckling of Dr. Marquez.

Finally, even his laughter died down, and Dr. Marquez said: "For a moment there I thought I was at the Council of Nicaea, and I thought of all the blood split over the difference between *homoousios* and *homoiousios*." Everyone looked at him dumbfounded, but still silent. He went on to explain: "Was the Son of the 'same substance' or 'similar substance' to the Father. That one letter, 'i,' caused so many problems for us as a Church." Dr. Marquez chuckled again; the others still stared at him, stupefied. "And we have a bigger problem than those at Nicaea. Where they were divided over one letter, we're divided over four." Again Dr. Marquez laughed, and again the others sat confounded. "Their 'i' has become our 's-h-i-t.' Now, brothers and sisters, are we going to allow this one word to divide our community and prolong this meeting?"

The eye of the storm passed, and a dangerous eyewall emerged as both sides began once again to hurl violent accusations at one another. Dr. Marquez smiled and calmly raised his hand. The room again fell silent, and he said, "I see this fundraiser is beginning to be more trouble than it's worth. I'd rather surrender one million dollars than have it divide our community. Now one of two things can happen. I can either cancel the fundraiser all together, or we can work together to find a solution that satisfies both sides."

"Holy shit, Doc," exclaimed one of the members of the old guard, "we've been here comin' on two hours of debate. There ain't no compromising with these fundamentalists!"

Shouting down the swift objections of the holy rollers, Dr. Marquez slapped the table hard and cried out: "Now that's brilliant! Brilliant! Why didn't I think of that? You've just saved the fundraiser!"

Everyone looked at Dr. Marquez in great surprise and anticipation. "*Holy* shit." Before the holy rollers could object, but not before they let out a collective gasp, Dr. Marquez quickly explained: "Our God is so great and loving, *everything* he creates is good. He himself says so in *Genesis*. Even shit. You've just made a profound philosophical insight."

"What are you saying, Doc?" asked members from both sides in unison.

"Our fundraiser," he replied, "is going to be called 'Chicken Shit Bingo.' It's appropriate, and it sends a necessary message to the community at large in our divisive times. Everything, every person is holy. Nothing is excluded from God's salvific plan. Nothing. Not even shit."

"And pieces of shit," replied a member of the old guard, looking directly at one of the holy rollers.

Chapter 11

By now, thoroughly exhausted, Dr. Marquez saw the members of the Alumni and Supporters Committee out the front doors. He said his goodbyes to each member as they made their way to their vehicles. Dr. Marquez locked up, waddled to his own truck, and drove the four blocks home, eagerly looking forward to a nightcap and bed. Rarely had he felt this tired.

He parked his truck, slowly opened the door, and plopped a heavy foot down on the concrete with a thud. He began the final dozen or so steps toward the front door and blissful rest, lifted his leonine head and saw his neighbor sitting on the porch.

"Gotta talk to you, Frank."

Annoyance, irritation, disillusion, dejection all welled up inside him. His heart sank into his stomach and his soul let out a stream of profanities, but his mouth ejected only a "Sure, Terry. What's up?" and then curled into an inviting smile.

"You know I stopped drinking two nights ago."

"I did not, but I'm glad to hear it." Dr. Marquez opened the front door and held it until Terry entered.

The two made their way to the living room. "Would you like some sweet tea, Terry? Left over enchiladas?"

"Nah, Frank. I just want my mind to stop racing. Every time I stop, I get all jittery and my mind moves a hundred and ten miles an hour."

"It sounds like you got it bad, Terry. But it also sounds par for the course. You stay the course, and each day will get just a little bit easier. Of course, these next couple of weeks are going to be the toughest you've ever been through, but you'll see I'm right—things will gradually start to get better."

"I don't know, Doc. You know I've tried religion. Ever since I went on that ACTS retreat three years ago. But I got my demons, too. I get things going, and then those bastards rear their ugly heads and I'm back to step one. I pray every day for help, but I'm not sure my prayers are doin' much good."

"I see."

"I feel like its God who's forcin' my hand. I ask for help, and he ignores me. I want the grace to stop drinking, but he won't give it to me, and so I keep drinkin'. I remember him sayin', 'ask and ye shall receive.' Well, I been askin' and haven't received nuthin. He don't give a shit, and that's why I drink!"

Dr. Marquez nodded, folded his hands, looked toward the ceiling, and sighed. "Sometimes, I feel the same way. All he has to do is give me grace, just a little, and I could conquer my own demons. I know what you're going through, Terry. I've got a thorn in my side, too, that I've begged God to remove. Over and over. I hate my thorn, and sometimes it makes me hate myself. But I do trust him, and know it's for a reason."

"Fuck that bullshit answer, Doc! I've been prayin' to him for three years and askin' for help four years before that. All I get is bullshit silence! Why not help me now? Right goddamn fuckin' now?!"

"I don't know, Terry. But I promise you, there's a beautiful reason he sometimes withholds grace. Sometimes for years."

"Shiiit…like what? What could possibly justify his abandonment of one of his own?"

"Maybe he's trying to keep you from a worse sin."

"The hell's that mean?"

"Well, hear me out now. It might be that he's allowed you continue in your current sin—alcoholism—so that you don't commit a more serious one. Now hold on, Terry, and let me explain. Now you're addicted to carnal pleasure, a sin of the flesh. If you were given enough grace all at once to overcome it, and if you defeated your addiction too easily, you might fall into the far more serious sin of pride. Maybe it's necessary for you to learn humility. The fact is that you can't do this on your own. By withholding grace, he is teaching you how weak you are. It's forcing you to live in reality."

"What're sayin', Doc? I should be grateful for my alcoholism? Bullshit."

"No, not at all. In fact, it might send you to hell. You need to defeat it. And sooner than later. But the first step is humility."

"I'm definitely humble, Frank. Seven years of battling this demon has definitely taught me humility."

"So, you're more humble than most?"

"Yep."

"Are you proud of that fact?"

"Go to hell, Frank. I got the point."

"All right, now you got to learn to talk…"

"Funny, Doc. I certainly have the gift of gab."

"…to him."

"I pray to him every damn day. I told you that. Seven years worth of prayin'."

"I mean conversating, Terry. Do you have conversations with him?"

"I pray the Rosary every now and then, get to Mass sometimes, and say my 'Our Fathers,' do the Litany of the Saints…"

"Conversation, Terry. Do you have *conversations* with him, or do you do all the talking?"

"What does that mean?"

"It sounds to me like you say your prayers, but you need to learn to be a pray-er."

"Speak plain, Frank."

"Again, I don't know you all that well, Terry, and I might be wrong…"

"Spit it out, Doc."

"Well, it sounds like you might be giving God a laundry list of petitions. 'Give me grace for this. Give me grace for that.' You got the petition part down. You got to learn to thank him, intercede, and adore. You see, Terry, prayer is a relationship. And your relationship is shit right now because it's a one-way street. You talking, no, you demanding to be heard. But do you listen?"

"The hell with that! You're sayin' God made me an alcoholic because he wants me to *talk* to him more? Screw that! I got a wife, or had one. I don't need another. Either you got it all wrong, Doc, or that God of yours is one needy motherfucker."

"He is needy, Terry. He needs your love, and love starts with conversations, with honest two-way conversations.

"I think you're full of shit, Frank! I'm an alcoholic because God wants to talk?! Well, shit." Terry got up in a fury and began to stomp toward the front door.

"No, Terry. You're an alcoholic because you don't want to be sober."

Terry whipped around, and in two steps closed to punching range as Dr. Marquez struggled to heave his substantial bulk out of his chair. He finally managed and stood facing a red-faced, chest-heaving, fist-clenched, lip-quivering madman.

"Don't want to get sober? Seven years! Seven fucking years!! Seven, goddamn, fucking years, Frank!!! And I don't *want* to get sober?!? I'm a drunk because some pussy in the sky wants me to share my feelings?!"

"No, Terry. Your seven years of hell have brought you closer to him. You've endured the tough times. You're still talking to him—not listening, but at least talking. He appreciates that. And he trusts you. Think about it, Terry. Seven years, no grace—at least not that you can see—and you're still on his side. He's teaching you to suffer, and so far, you've been strong enough. There's only one step left. One step, Terry. One step, and you can do it."

Terry stood glaring at him, one instant from assault, maybe worse. Dr. Marquez stared right back with compassionate, calm eyes.

"Go to rehab, Terry."

Terry's shoulders slumped. He had heard this before. From his wife. From his two children. From his friends. It was the last thing he wanted to hear from Dr. Marquez.

"I can't, Doc. You don't understand, you're not from here. This is a hard community to live in. There's no hiding a stint in rehab."

"Do you really, *really* want to get better, Terry?"

Terry's chin hit his chest, and he began to sob silently, and then audibly. "Yes, Doc, you know I want to.... I want these demons... gone. There's a legion of them and ...I...can't take it anymore. I want help, but...I'm scared, Doc. Real scared. I don't know if I can."

"You can, Terry. You can, and then those demons will leave you. Pray with me, will you?"

And then Dr. Marquez and Terry, his alcoholic neighbor, dropped to their knees and uttered a joint, cathartic supplication. Ten minutes later, Terry was in his pickup truck on his way to a rehab clinic. Dr. Marquez was right behind him.

Chapter 12

His first semester had been a success. After tightening the school's belt and enlarging his own, Dr. Marquez was ten pounds heavier, and the school's debt was considerably lighter. It had required some difficult and unpopular decisions: releasing popular but ineffective staff, assigning those he kept extra duties, and becoming a full-time teacher himself, in addition to his extensive administrative duties.

Dr. Marquez was frequently seen running the carpool line, serving food in the cafeteria, proctoring the chess club, tutoring struggling students in all fields, teaching a weekend ACT prep course, and supervising the school liturgy schedule. Tonight, he would be attending the annual Christmas program and was thus engaged in hauling around Christmas trees and wreaths to be set up as decorations.

At 5:30, parents, grandparents, and kin began pouring into the church. Dr. Marquez held the doors and greeted each entry with well wishes and his infectious laugh. At 6:05, he mounted the ambo, addressed the audience, and wished the various grade choirs good luck.

He descended into his pew and proceeded to enjoy a wonderful program that included *Silent Night, The First Noel, We Three Kings, Hark! The Herald Angels Sing, O Little Town of Bethlehem, O Come, O Come, Emmanuel,* and *Frosty the Snowman.* He thought the singing was adequate in the lowest grades, pleasant from fourth to sixth grade, awkward in the middle grades, and beautiful once the high school choir took over. All in all, it was a successful evening...until he stood up to thank the choir, choir director, parent volunteers, and give his concluding remarks. A full one-quarter of the audience had left. What had happened, he wondered? Surely, the performance was not unlike the school's past programs?

He returned to his school office after waddling down the sidewalk, sharing pleasantries with some parents, receiving embarrassed looks from others, and the occasional lowered head that vacillated in disgust.

He plopped into his chair, crossed his feet at the ankles, fired up his computer, signed into his e-mail, and then he understood.

A secular song had been song in God's holy house, and in front of the Blessed Presence no less.

The congregation had been duped into worshipping not a golden calf but a sentient, soulless monstrosity of packed snow. The House of God was to be a house of prayer, but Dr. Marquez and his choir had turned it into a den of idolatry. And for what? To pay homage to a three-tiered demon with coal-black eyes! Several parishioners and supporters of Holy Family had decided to band together and cease their tithing. They would not support a church that whored itself to secular deities.

Dr. Marquez sat back and took a deep breath. And then he let loose such a howl of laughter that the blinds in his office shook. He laughed boisterously for several minutes and then he shut down his computer and began the laborious task of getting up from his seat and preparing to go home. He would deal with the *Frosty* schismatics tomorrow—when he was in a less jovial and more somber mood. Fr. Pat, although he would certainly back up Dr. Marquez, would not take too kindly to the loss of any parishioner's tithe.

The next morning Dr. Marquez sent out a mass e-mail to his faculty requesting that the *Frosty* fiasco not be discussed publicly, and to the community at large explaining that last night's Christmas program did indeed contain secular songs, but that the Sacred Host had been removed from the tabernacle. He gave a brief exegesis on the historical role of Catholic churches, including their history as places of worship and meeting houses. He explained the difference between the Church and church. He concluded by congratulating the choirs for their beautiful performance and thanking the concerned citizens of Wilhelmsburg for their piety and devotion to the sanctity of God's house. The beauty and holiness of the community could not be sustained without the children, the choir director, and those who kept such a vigilant eye on liturgical piety, for they were the modern-day Maccabees. Dr. Marquez knew his tormenters would fail to grasp this latter reference. Secretly, he thought them unworthy of the name Maccabee and more deserving of the epithet Guelph or Jacobin.

Chapter 13

Dr. Marquez was enjoying the Knights of Columbus Red River Shootout Christmas Classic, an eight team post-Christmas basketball tournament. Holy Family had won the first game, lost the second, and was now playing in the consolation game. He was pleased to see that while Holy Family's fans were borderline excessive in their enthusiasm, their vulgarities had been kept out of earshot. Not even Hoss Schilling was violating appropriate fan protocol. Dr. Marquez attended nearly all Holy Family's home games and a handful of the road games, mostly to keep an eye on the passionate fans. His constant presence had been a reminder to them that sportsmanship extended to the bleachers as well.

The game ended in a 37-46 defeat. The fans began piling out dejected and frustrated. The players got scolded in the locker room and then left carefree and young and looking forward to getting back to Wilhelmsburg and the rest of their Christmas break.

Dr. Marquez congratulated the boys on their effort and then began making his own way to the packed parking lot. Because the game was only thirteen miles from Wilhelmsburg, the players were allowed to drive themselves to and from the game. Now they began piling into cars by twos and threes, laughing and making plans for the rest of the night. Most of the parents had already left skulking and bitter.

[Two hours earlier.

"Are you sure you want to park here?"

"Why not?"

"You're on the edge of a ditch."

"There's nowhere else to park. You can get through my door if you need to."

"I can hop down. It's your van I was worried about. I don't want it to get stuck while we're at the game."

"It'll be fine. Let's go."]

Two hours later, it was not fine. As they left the game and approached the impromptu parking lot, they noticed their ride home was leaning awkwardly to the right. When they got closer, they saw the right side tires had sunk into the soft grass. They both climbed in the van from the driver's side, started the engine, put it in drive, and sat still as the tires rapidly churned. They put it in reverse and again sat still as the tires spun at six thousand rotations a minute. No doubt about it—they were stuck.

"Dammit. What do we do now?"

"I think you're going to need a tow truck, man."

Something immediately dropped into the pit of his stomach causing it to tighten. He thought about how stupid he had been to park there in the first place. He had plans tonight and now he would be stuck up here trying to get his van out of a ditch. He thought of the embarrassment of having to tell his father, of the Monday morning laughter at school, and of the expense of a tow truck. His mind filled with disgusted and angry thoughts.

Not knowing what to do, he did what he always did when he was in trouble: he called his father. His father was the last person he wanted to explain this recent mistake to, but also the first person he always called when he was in a bind.

He pulled out his phone, dialed home, and asked his father to come to the high school because the van he had allowed his son to take out that night was stuck in a ditch. He wanted to end the conversation as quickly as possible; he just wanted his father to be there.

"Okay. Sit tight. I'll be there in fifteen minutes."

He let out a sigh of relief. He was at the point of no return. His father knew he had done something stupid. Hopefully the fifteen-minute drive would give him time to cool down and not anger him more.

"Goddammit! Why didn't he listen? I told him the car was on the edge of a damn ditch. If he wasn't so damn stubborn, we'd be on the way to the party now." Hayden stood there beside his friend. The parking lot was emptying, but he could still catch a ride with one of his less stubborn friends who had not parked their car in a ditch. He was tempted to do so. Who knew how long it would take to tow the van back unto the road? By then the party would be halfway over. He looked at his distraught friend and then looked beyond him at the last dozen or so cars in the parking lot. Only a few more belonged to his friends. If he was going to get to the party, now was the time to catch that ride.

Dr. Marquez noticed two of his students still at the stadium standing by the road. Most had already cleared out, but these two remained. Then he saw the van and understood. He veered away from the path that would take him to his own safely parked truck and headed toward his students.

"Hi, Dr. Marquez," spoke the tall one in a humbled tone.

"Brady."

Dr. Marquez's doctoral classes and long hours of observation and contemplation had taught him much about the human psyche. He knew that stating the obvious would only embarrass his student further. He was a teenager, after all; he probably had a cell phone and had already made the necessary calls. All Dr. Marquez needed to do was stay and wait with them until help arrived.

Why wasn't his father here by now? Didn't he know how embarrassing this was? Now his principal and a couple of his teachers knew he had let his van tumble into a ditch. If his father would just hurry up and get here, he would know how to get the van out of the ditch, and he could get to the party and forget about this humiliating episode—at least until Monday. "HURRY THE HELL UP!" he inwardly screamed.

But as the fifteen minutes got closer and closer, he began to panic. The knot in his stomach was beginning to tighten and his heart beat faster. How angry would his father be? What would he say to his foolish son? He began to think up excuses as to how the van ended up in the ditch. Quickly, he realized he had none.

His palms became sticky. His stomach started to hurt. All he wanted was to be at home in his bed facing the wall with the covers over his head. Any minute now. Any minute now.

Hayden thought to himself: "I could have been there by now." But then he looked over at his nervous friend and realized he had to be here. Why? He didn't know, but he had to. The only thing worse than being here right now would be to not be here. He could be at the party, but he wouldn't be having any fun. A distressed friend had some sort of pull that always kept him nearby. He didn't want to be here, but he chose to be here. Somehow, deep down, he knew he was doing a more important work than the tow truck that would soon put his friend's van back on the road. He knew he couldn't solve the problem, but at least he could share in the problem. And so he stayed.

After about fifteen minutes a car pulled up. Dr. Marquez recognized it as belonging to the father of his student. "Now things should get interesting," he thought. He wondered how the father was going to react when he saw the van. What would he say? He had seen similar situations many times before: a disobedient or foolish or stubborn child and an angry father. His student would probably get a well-deserved tongue-lashing. And why not? He deserved it for treating his father's property so carelessly. He looked over at his student, saw his panic, and began to feel sorry for him.

The suspense was coming to an end. The father pulled up and parked about thirty feet from the van. The door opened and a foot stepped out onto the pavement. "Well, here it comes," thought Dr. Marquez. He knew the father would be angry, would probably even shout at his foolish son. He just hoped the episode would be over quickly.

The second foot hit the pavement, and a head slowly rose above the car door. The figure began walking toward the van. But it was not an angry face that approached. Nor was it upset or disappointed. Instead, it was a smiling face.

He walked up to his son and the smile never faded. He put his arm around his child, and the smile was still there. He told him it wasn't a big deal, that stuff like this happens. And still, the smile.

Dr. Marquez couldn't believe it. The van was right there. In a ditch. The guilty son was standing by it. And his father greeted him with a pat on the back and a smile!?

All his anxiety, all the tension in his stomach dissolved like water and poured out of him when he saw his father's smile. Shame and warmth and gratitude coursed through his body.

Many years later, reflecting on that night, he had forgotten the conversations and the tow truck and the party. All he remembered was a smile and a father's mercy.

Dr. Marquez, too, would spend much time reflecting on this parable-turned-reality.

Chapter 14

The Spring semester began in a highly unusual way. Not unusually, it began with controversy. It had been a bitter, cold winter thus far, and the local weather experts were predicting an icy, dangerous January. The students were looking forward to four or five or maybe even six snow days, even though they had just come off a two-and-a-half week break.

Despite the sub-freezing weather, Mrs. Danielle Gottlieb, one of Holy Family's moms, came to the school in a risqué, low-cut blouse that exposed much of her ample bosom. The frigid weather outside made her bra-less ensemble even more scandalous.

As luck would have it, Mrs. Thelma Pruitt was entering the building at the same time to complain about the lack of student participation in Mass earlier that morning. The two women made eye contact. Mrs. Pruitt returned Mrs. Gottlieb's smile by lowering and shaking her head, then raising her head and scowling. Mrs. Gottlieb wondered what had gotten into Mrs. Pruitt as she continued down the hall and walked out the front doors of the school toward her stylish black SUV. Mrs. Horvath's eighth grade class was just coming back from Music class, boys and girls intermingled. Some of the boys stopped to tie their shoes, some slowed down to kick acorns off the sidewalk while others simply slackened their pace. By the time Mrs. Gottlieb raised her long left leg into her SUV and reached over with her left hand to shut the door, exposing more of her bounteous bosom in the process, all the eighth grade girls were inside. The boys had not been in such a hurry, and they now gazed longingly at the derriere of the SUV as it drove off.

In a white hot fury, Mrs. Pruitt stormed into Dr. Marquez' office. The lack of participation at morning Mass was by now a distant memory. Mrs. Pruitt had found a new crusade: drive the blasphemous siren from the sanctified grounds of God's school.

"Dr. Marquez, I find it highly inappropriate the way some of our parents dress while on campus!"

"Good morning, Mrs. Pruitt. It's good to see you again. I couldn't help but admire your singing this morning at Mass. I always feel that I get more uplifted when you're cantoring." He was trying to steer her away from a discussion of Mrs. Gottlieb's wardrobe and toward some aspect of Mass that he was sure she had found fault with. He failed.

"Dr. Marquez, I sing to bring glory to God. I also dress in a way that honors him."

"And you do honor him with your song. I particularly enjoyed your rendition of *On Eagle's Wings.*"

"Dr. Marquez, it's simply scandalous to allow some of the outfits our parents wear on campus. And with all these teenage boys around! It just can't happen."

"I couldn't agree more, Mrs. Pruitt. Now, are you going to be singing at any of our Masses next week?"

"Dr. Marquez, we can discuss my singing at the appropriate time. At the moment, we really must do something about our parents' dress code. I don't want my children going to a school where they're exposed to living, walking pornography!"

"Mrs. Pruitt, what do you mean by that?"

"Thigh high skirts, Barbie-Doll hair, exposed chests."

"Now who would you be referring to? I haven't noticed any short skirts around campus."

"I can't tell you how happy I am to hear that, Dr. Marquez. But I guarantee you the unmarried boys in this school, our students I mean, do notice it. Our married men don't notice that stuff anymore—I know, I'm married to one—but the students do. One of the beauties of marriage is that it stifles the you-know-what drive. But our boy students don't yet have the grace to resist such temptations. Their hormones are raging. And when you allow scantily clad women to wander our halls at will, you give those hormones free reign. If one of our students had just seen what I just saw, and, God forbid, were to be struck by a car while walking home this afternoon, his soul would be in real danger. We need to make sure attending our Catholic school is not a threat to their salvation."

Dr. Marquez had listened, amused by Mrs. Pruitt's soliloquy. "I appreciate your concern for the mores of our school family, and I couldn't agree with you more. It's imperative that we set an example in our own dress. Now, I assure you that if I see any of our parents on school grounds dressed inappropriately, I'll address the situation immediately."

"God bless, you, Dr. Marquez, but you seem to be awfully naïve. Sin has been right under your nose. Within your grasp. And you let it escape."

"What are you referring to, Mrs. Pruitt?"

"Dr. Marquez…*she* was just here."

"Who?"

"The spawn of Astarte."

"If I'm to handle this situation, I'll need to know exactly who you're referring to, Mrs. Pruitt."

Mrs. Pruitt looked over her shoulder, out the window, and over her shoulder again before whispering: "You know…*her*… Mrs. Gottlieb."

Dr. Marquez feigned ignorance. "Yes, Mrs. Gottlieb was just here dropping off her tuition. Early, as usual."

"Dr. Marquez!" Mrs. Pruitt exclaimed in exasperation.

"Yes, Mrs. Pruitt?"

"Don't tell me you didn't notice her attire."

Dr. Marquez squinted his eyes and looked to the ceiling as if trying to remember the scene in his office minutes before. "Now that you mention Mrs. Gottlieb, I do recall her voice sounding a little hoarse. I sure hope she's not coming down with anything. Especially with those little ones she's got running around at home…."

"Dr. Marquez! Her clothes! Her outfits! Her blouses! Her exposed and pendulous bosom!" Mrs. Pruitt gasped and quickly raised her hand to her mouth. The word "bosom" was foreign to her vocabulary on account of its vulgarity. Now, she was madder than ever. That hussy had forced her into a profane utterance.

Calmly, she lowered her hand and said in an even, controlled voice: "Dr. Marquez, it is imperative that you not allow that woman to prance around our school in her skimpy outfits. She is turning Holy Family into a veritable Red Light District."

"Well, Mrs. Pruitt, I simply did not notice her outfit. I sure am glad you brought it to my attention. I simply would have let the matter pass through ignorance. Now I can address the issue. Luckily for our school, we have a watch dog like you."

"I'm just a mouthpiece of the Lord's will. Like Mother Teresa claims, a pencil in the hand of God. I'm grateful and humble that He's chosen me to protect our children from such indecent influences."

"As I said, we're all lucky to have you. Now, what I propose to do is this: I'm going to send out a mass e-mail to our entire school community, reminding

them that it is our Christian duty to present ourselves—and the way we dress—as children of God,
especially while on campus. That means dressing
with humility and propriety. If a parent again comes
on campus dressed in an inappropriate way, then I'll
give them a choice: they can immediately leave campus and come back when they're dressed more mod-
estly, or they can cover up with an extra-large, black
trash bag that I'll keep handy beside my desk. I think
the fear of wearing a Catholic burqa will deter any
inappropriate dress."

Mrs. Pruitt was delighted with Dr. Marquez's decision. She thanked him for his zeal in cleansing the
school of its Jezebels and gloatingly walked toward
her car hoping to run into Mrs. Gottlieb again.

Dr. Marquez sat at his desk, watched Mrs. Pruitt
climb into her car, shut the door, and drive off. Only
then did he let forth the joyous, boisterous laugh that
had become his trademark. His solution had been
perfect, for he knew that Mrs. Pruitt did not use e-
mail due to inappropriate spam messages her oldest
son had received six or seven years ago. The boy had
tried to explain that such spam messages were una-
voidable and were sent at random. She did not

believe him. She cancelled her internet, and the boy was sent to a summer camp that specialized in healing the lustful, pornographers, fornicators, and homosexuals. Thus, Dr. Marquez was assured that any e-mail he sent would not reach Mrs. Pruitt. He spent the next ten minutes writing up a general e-mail reminding students, faculty, and parents of the student dress code.

Chapter 15

Dr. Marquez sat at a table enjoying a plate of parmesan garlic wings with a side of loaded potato skins. The waitress had just removed the cleaned plate that had recently been home to a Big Jack Daddy Burger and a House Sampler. Another plate—Cheesecake Bites—was on its way.

It had been a good meal, made better by the company. Raul Lopez sat at the other end of the booth. He had been a friend of Dr. Marquez ever since Dr. Marquez had first visited him at the Monroe City Prison. Raul had been locked up for six months for possession of marijuana. After his release two months ago, he had secured a job as a janitor at the abortion clinic forty-five minutes south-east of Wilhelmsburg. To the people of Wilhelmsburg, the clinic was a veritable Gehenna, the personification of evil, the lair of Satan himself.

Dr. Marquez had visited the Monroe prison as one of his numerous corporal works of mercy. He and Raul connected, and Dr. Marquez had agreed to become his confirmation sponsor when Raul made it clear that he wished to turn away from the streets and return to the practice of Catholicism in which his mother had raised him.

To Ms. Inez Lopez, Raul's mother, Dr. Marquez was a Godsend. She had already had him over to dinner twice and had begged him to continue to be in Raul's life, even, and especially, after he was released from prison. Dr. Marquez had given his word to do so, and now he and Raul broke chicken wings together.

They talked about baseball, home-cooking, the challenges of growing up poor, the importance of a relationship with Jesus, and were discussing a DVD Dr. Marquez had gifted to Raul, *There Be Dragons*, when Daniel Wolf, Mrs. Pruitt's son-in-law, caught sight of Dr. Marquez from across the restaurant and walked over to say hello.

He approached the table with his right hand beginning to extend itself to Dr. Marquez's side when he saw Raul. He started ever so slightly knowing that he knew that face. Not being able to place where he had seen Raul before, Daniel shook Dr. Marquez's hand and was exchanging a few pleasantries when a sudden shuddering horror convulsed his spine. That man seated across from Dr. Marquez was the janitor at the abortion clinic!

Daniel stared at him to be sure, and then, sure, glared at him with all the malice he could muster. Having seen Daniel protesting outside the clinic every Saturday and two other evenings each week since he had taken the job, Raul sat there hoping not to be recognized. Now he lowered his head in embarrassment.

"*You*?!" Daniel spewed in contempt.

Raul sheepishly raised his head and attempted a slight smile. He offered his hand and promptly returned it to his lap when it too was glared at in contempt.

Daniel then turned his betrayed and bitter eyes to Dr. Marquez. "I must say, Dr. Marquez, I am surprised." He then turned to leave. After a few steps he turned around and added, "and disappointed."

Daniel returned to his table across the room, helped his wife clean up the faces of his two youngest children, got a to-go box for the leftovers, and called for the check. He refused to sit down until the check came. When it came, he pulled out his cell phone for its calculator app, and typed in "56.73 x .09", his customary 9% tip that assured God's tithe would be higher. After seeing his tab would come to $61.83, he decided he oughtn't tip a restaurant that would open its doors to abortion clinic workers. He signed his name on the receipt, leaving the tip line blank, picked up his youngest child and stalked out the restaurant. On the way out he glanced over one last time at the table of Dr. Marquez and Raul hoping to murder them with his eyes, especially Raul, but the two were laughing, Raul silently with his head down, Dr. Marquez boisterously with his head rolled back. Daniel was certain that Raul had just told Dr. Marquez a joke about some babies he had helped butcher at the clinic. He walked out the front double doors fuming. When he got to his car, he had his wife buckle the children in as he called his mother-in-law.

Chapter 16

Dr. Marquez had enjoyed his dinner with Raul. He was happy to see that the young man was getting his life together. Raul even had a lead on a job as a janitor at Monroe's movie theater. Dr. Marquez prayed he would get that job. He even mused over the possibility of hiring him at Holy Family but couldn't envision any maintenance position opening up. Regardless, he was confident that something would come Raul's way.

When Dr. Marquez turned the last corner and approached his house, he saw a line of cars parked down the street. He immediately deduced two possibilities: his neighbor Terry had had an accident, or a Pruitt-led lynch mob awaited him. The lack of an ambulance told him it was the latter. In that case, an ambulance might be needed shortly.

He parked, and the crowd immediately made its way to his car. He opened the door, and the crowd moved closer. He hefted his left leg and prepared to step down, and the crowd stepped back. He landed safely, didn't tumble over, and the crowd, no longer fearing being crushed themselves, surged toward Dr.

Marquez, threatening to crush him against his truck. Half a dozen voices shouted at him all at once. Dr. Marquez braced himself against his truck, held up his two hands, extended his palms upward, and began laughing. His calmness, frivolity, and booming laugh temporarily silenced the mob.

"In High School, I hit a game winning RBI triple against Deion Sanders, and the crowds were excited to see me, but not *this* excited. What happened? Did I win the lottery while I was out this evening?" He laughed even harder at his joke, and the mob stood there. "I'm curious for the reason for this celebratory greeting. I feel like Caesar returning from Gaul." There was more laughter, but just from himself. "I would invite you all in for some ice cream, but I regrettably bought just two gallons last night. You might not believe it, but despite my trim physique, I have quite an appetite, and there's not enough left to share with everyone." The sound of his lonely laughter filled the chill night air again.

Finally, Mrs. Pruitt stepped forward and exclaimed, "We know where you were tonight, Dr. Marquez. More to the point, we know *who* you were with." She turned to the crowd and shouted, "This man was dining with the worst of all sinners…an ABORTION CLINIC DOCTOR!" The mob, already having been told the story and consisting of six of her own children and a number of ladies Mrs. Pruitt had unofficially appointed co-watchdogs, howled in disapproval.

Dr. Marquez laughed again and said, "I assure you vigilant sisters in Christ that I was not eating with an abortion doctor. I know lots of people in lots of fields, but to this day, I can say I don't know any abortion doctors personally."

His denial only fueled their rage. "We know you were there. We saw you!"

"Now, good people, I came straight home, how could you all have seen me when I didn't see any of you where I was. And how could you all have gotten to my house and organized before I arrived?"

Mrs. Pruitt took the initiative again: "Stop playing games with us, Dr. Marquez. *We* weren't there, of course, but my son-in-law, Daniel was, and he told us everything."

"I did see Daniel this evening. In fact, I tried to introduce him to my friend, Raul, but I think he was in a hurry to get back to his wife and kids at his own table."

"He told us *everything*, Dr. Marquez. You're the principal of our school, of our *Catholic* school. How can you eat with such people? And in public, too?!?"

Dr. Marquez sighed, but still with a smile on his face. "Although I regrettably cannot entertain everyone here, perhaps, Mrs. Pruitt, we could speak inside a moment. You, me, and just a few more."

"Why not answer for yourself here, now...in front of all of us?"

"Because, Mrs. Pruitt, even Pilate allowed private audiences with those he was to condemn."

Mrs. Pruitt, not quite catching the reference, was delighted that Dr. Marquez had equated himself with Pontius Pilate. In a grand gesture of magnanimity, she agreed to play the role of Christ and enter into the pagan's palatial home. She and three co-zealots agreed to speak with Dr. Marquez in the privacy of his home.

As soon as Dr. Marquez shut the front door behind his interlocutors, Mrs. Pruitt immediately got to the point: "So, Dr. Marquez, why were you dining with abortion doctors?"

Instead of answering Mrs. Pruitt directly, Dr. Marquez began with a question of his own: "Do you recall, Mrs. Pruitt, the story in Luke of a woman crying on our Savior's feet?"

She looked at him with narrowed eyes and with clenched teeth.

"Or maybe the early life of Saul, or Augustine…Francis…Ignatius?"

Her eyes and teeth both tightened even more.

"What I'm trying to say, Mrs. Pruitt, is that we need to always remember the power of forgiveness, and that people can change…."

"*Some* people can change," she interrupted. "It seems to me, Dr. Marquez, that you plan to water down our faith and the faith of our children."

"By no means, Mrs. Pruitt. I only want to keep an open mind and open heart when dealing with others. I want to treat people like my hero treated the sinful woman weeping on his feet. Or the lamb who was lost."

"Thank God he did not give you the keys to the Kingdom of Heaven; you would let *everyone* in."

"And thank God he did not give you the keys to the Gates of Hell; everyone but you would be there,"

Dr. Marquez thought, but he said, "No, Mrs. Pruitt, he gave them to another sinful but forgiven man."

Mrs. Pruitt, not wishing to continue the interrogation at the moment, huffed and walked to the door, posse in tow. At the door she turned around and spewed, "You're on a slippery slope, Doctor, and you're dragging the Holy Family community down with you. By this time next year, we'll have the abortion doctor in Dallas as our school nurse, performing abortions in your office!"

Chapter 17

The previous night's soiree had reached the ears of Father Pat, and Dr. Marquez prepared to defend his actions again. He traveled to the rectory first thing in the morning, at 6:00, to meet with Fr. Pat before he had to begin preparing for 8:00 Mass.

Expecting to be warned about his choice of friends, Dr. Marquez had thought about preparing a defense but decided to roll the die and speak with Fr. Pat unprepared and frankly.

Fr. Pat was at the front door, waiting, and opened it before Dr. Marquez could knock.

"I hear the hounds treed a coon last night, Frank."

"More like a walrus, Father."

"Ha! They ought to be careful. A walrus falling out of a tree can do a lot of damage to those staring up hoping to see its demise."

Now Dr. Marquez laughed. And then laughed some more, which in turn made Fr. Pat's chuckle morph into open laughter. He quickly caught himself and motioned Dr. Marquez in quickly. He shut the door and said, "I might be visited by a mob myself now."

"I'm sorry, Father, I should have come in the back door."

"No, no, not that. I was standing on the porch speaking with the town's chief sinner and laughing boisterously. You see, they expect me to invite you over and chastise you. Perhaps even excommunicate you. Some, I dare say are hoping you leave the rectory in an ambulance having been stoned to death by their beloved priest. No one expects me to *laugh* with you. In fact, many feel as if a priest should not laugh at all."

"I've always found sour Catholics a confusing breed, Father."

"Yes, yes. Sometimes, I wonder if they really believe. I mean *really* believe. If they claim to believe in the atoning value of Jesus' death and that a sacramental life will end in heaven, how can they be such Debbie Downers?"

"Hahaha! I agree with you, Father. I have two paintings in my office, you'll recall. One of my favorite Bible stories, *The Road to Emmaus*, and the other of Jesus throwing back his head laughing."

"Yes, I've noticed. And why shouldn't he laugh. He had friends. Not just disciples and apostles, and followers, but *friends*. And he lived a fully emotional human life. So, yes, he must have laughed countless times. The problem with our community is that they only want to see Christ Crucified. They don't want a laughing Lord. It offends their sensibilities."

"I've often reflected on that picture, Father, and I wonder what made him toss back his head and laugh so hard. What situation is he laughing at, or what joke and who told it?"

"Oh, I don't know. If you twisted my arm and made me guess, I would say Peter. He seems to have been quite a character."

"Hahaha! I always thought of Peter as the Apostolic Forrest Gump."

Father Pat shook his head and chuckled. "I haven't heard that one before, but that's good...an interesting comparison." He chuckled again and both men sat quietly for a while. Fr. Pat then told Dr. Marquez about his own recent run in with the Catholic Taliban.

"I was on my porch last month watering my flowers one Saturday morning. I heard the phone ring and then ring again, and then again. Assuming it must be an emergency, I set my watering can down and went inside to check my messages. It was Mrs. Goering calling. She wanted me to know I had forgotten to put my pants on."

Dr. Marquez looked quizzically at Fr. Pat.

"You see, I was watering my flowers in my shorts. Knee-length, blue-jean shorts to be specific. She was scandalized that a priest would wear anything but the traditional priestly long, black pants."

Dr. Marquez then erupted into a paroxysm of laughter, accompanied by Fr. Pat's much softer chuckle. Dr. Marquez understood now why he had been called over to the rectory. Rather than rebuking him, Fr. Pat had called the meeting as an act of solidarity.

Chapter 18

Just before Spring Break, another scandal erupted at Holy Family. Christine Haverkamp, a senior student, was pregnant. She had told the counselor, who in turn informed Dr. Marquez. She was only three months pregnant. The due date was mid-September, long after she graduated. However, she would inevitably start showing a bump sometime before Easter, a month and a half before graduation. She was destined to walk across the stage, receive her diploma, and shake the hand of the bishop with her enlarged belly.

Mrs. Pruitt had convinced the community that Christine and her belly would bring great shame to Holy Family. The bishop might even place the entire community under interdict. Her whoring and her belly would cause the citizens of Wilhelmsburg to be banned from the sacraments. No marriages, no baptisms, no Eucharist…for anyone. In short, Christine Haverkamp would bring hell to Wilhelmsburg and damnation to all those who died while under the bishop's interdiction. There was only one solution—don't let Christine graduate.

When Dr. Marquez approached his office on what should have been a routine Monday morning, more than a dozen concerned parents were waiting for him. He noticed with some surprise that this was a wide spectrum of parents, not just the usual zealots. Mrs. Pruitt's influence had evidently grown. Not surprisingly, these parents and grandparents had assembled to demand the immediate expulsion of Christine Haverkamp.

Immediately after his usual effusive greeting and smile, the parents laid it on thick. They indeed were calling for the removal of Christine from campus, effective immediately. At that moment, Christine herself walked by the mob. She was on her way to ask Dr. Marquez's permission to leave school every other Thursday afternoon thirty minutes early in order to have time to visit her OBGYN. She had come to the office at the wrong time. The mob instantly turned their venom on her. Some glared at her, some turned around in disgust, a select few openly taunted her. Just five seconds of this venom broke Christine. Dr. Marquez quietly and politely asked her to wait for him in his office. She walked by silently weeping, and the crowd began to pour in behind her. At this moment, Dr. Marquez deftly stepped behind Christine and stood in the doorway, thereby protecting her from the blood-thirsty mob with his immense bulk.

Suddenly, one of the mob, previously hidden by the other dozen or so, shouted out, "Fuckin' whore! Your bitchery is going to send all our unbaptized to hell!" With a sinking feeling, Dr. Marquez realized the voice could only belong to Hoss Schilling; it did. At first, Mrs. Pruitt and the elders of the Catholic Taliban cringed at his language. An unsummoned yet perversely delightful thought arose in Dr. Marquez: maybe Mrs. Pruitt would challenge Hoss regarding his language, Hoss would kill her by strangulation, and in turn be killed himself by Mrs. Pruitt's disciples. With blood on their hands, the old ladies of the Pruitt posse would flee toward the confessional allowing Christine Haverkamp to make her escape.

Dr. Marquez's fantasy appeared to be playing out when Mrs. Pruitt took two menacing steps toward Hoss. Dr. Marquez thought about intervening, but that would move him away from the door, thereby exposing Christine to clear and present danger.

Besides, he wanted to see if his premonition might turn into a blessing.

Suddenly, Mrs. Pruitt stopped, looked directly at Hoss, and exclaimed: "Well said, Judas Maccabeus!" Dr. Marquez couldn't believe his ears. Mrs. Pruitt had publicly allied herself with a man who represented everything she opposed: he was gruff, foul-mouthed, ill-dressed, ignorant, and went to Mass only on Easter and Christmas—and only if he wasn't too hung over from the night before. Clearly Hoss' drinking, womanizing, and blasphemy were only venially bad when compared with Christine's own shortcomings, which undoubtedly were of the mortal variety.

Dr. Marquez tried to calm the mob by promising to meet with them later in the day. They were not pacified. They intended to stay until Christine was escorted off campus, expulsion papers in hand, and they intended to do the escorting.

Suddenly, Mrs. Pruitt shouted out: "The case is clear, Dr. This hussy has been proven to be without any doubt a fornicator. You know our handbook. You know the penalty. Will you do your duty?"

Dr. Marquez was indeed familiar with the morality clause in the school's handbook. By letter of the law, Christine ought to be expelled. And yet, he couldn't bring himself to act so Draconian. After all, she could have terminated the pregnancy, and no one would have known. The secret would have died with her baby. Yet, she chose to brave the ridicule and scorn and perhaps worse of Wilhelmsburg to protect her young child. Dr. Marquez couldn't turn his back on her. Nor could he think of how to mollify the rabble.

His mind was frantically searching for a solution when Mrs. Pruitt called out again: "Enough lollygagging, Dr. Will you expel her or not? We're waiting for your answer. Are you not the principal? Are you even Catholic? Why the hesitation?"

Dr. Marquez, with measured words, slowly replied, "Very well. I'll go into my office now and draw up the paperwork expelling Christine this afternoon. But I would like each and every one of your signatures on the document as well. Fornication is a crime against not just the school but against the entire school family. Therefore, we all ought to sign the document. In addition, I believe this will set a wonderful precedent for Holy Family. No sin will be tolerated. *No* sin." As he said this, Dr. Marquez looked each antagonist in the eyes before continuing: "Furthermore, any violation of any of the Ten Commandments or Precepts of the Church or the School Handbook will henceforth be punishable by expulsion. Our own children and grandchildren will be the beneficiaries of this momentous occasion. Surely, word of Christine's expulsion will eliminate, once and for all, all school violations, from uniform infractions to teenage pregnancies. Holy Family will be a model of moral self-actualization. If no one can enter Heaven imperfect, no one will enter Holy Family in said condition of imperfectability. Have your pens ready, and I'll bring out the paperwork shortly."

Dr. Marquez waddled into his office leaving the quieted mob outside. He went to his computer, smiling at Christine as he passed. "Give me five minutes, and we'll chat, Miss Haverkamp. Things ought to be brighter then." Christine looked at him and wiped her eyes. Dr. Marquez sat at his computer and began typing an e-mail to his sister, pretending to hammer out the document that would assure Christine's expulsion.

Meanwhile, outside his office, the Pruitt posse was looking nervously at each other, especially those whose children and grandchildren had received detentions recently. A few drifted away.

Presently, Dr. Marquez emerged from his office excitedly waving a piece of recently printed com puter paper. "Great news, brothers and sisters! While I was in the office writing up our agreed upon document that will transform Holy Family into heaven on earth, I was hit by another sudden burst of inspiration…inspired, no doubt, by the Holy Spirit and you good people."

Some looked at him with pleased curiosity. How had the Holy Spirit used them to inspire Dr. Marquez? The majority, though, looked at him with worried apprehension, now fearing what the contract might say.

Dr. Marquez continued: "Your idea to enforce all the rules by any means necessary, not excluding expulsion, was brilliant. Of course, the enrollment at Holy Family will shrink at first, but I believe when the rest of Mississippi sees what we've become, saintly students and families will begin flocking to our community. We will be a veritable city upon a hill."

The crowd began to shift restlessly, both hoping and fearing he would get to the point.

He continued: "Why, brothers and sisters, should we stop the purification with our current students? Wouldn't that just be generational warfare? I propose we begin a careful winnowing of the Holy Family family *in toto*. Yes, why should previous generations get off scot-free? Let's purge our community, once and for all, of all vices, past and present? Let's set up a committee to separate the wheat from the chaff and expel violators current and past. Retroactively and posthumously!"

Only a select few applauded Dr. Marquez's new suggestion, and then only briefly. Some of the mob looked nervously around, the others lowered their eyes, drew in their shoulders, and tried to make themselves look smaller. Each began wondering if *they* would end up on that list. The older would-be persecutors began slipping away as quietly as possible.

Hoss Schilling recalled bedding Tiffany Hess under the bleachers during the homecoming dance, and

Bonnie Miller in the boys' locker room late one night, and Elmira Junker one Saturday evening in the science lab after he had made a copy of the classroom keys, unbeknownst to the school faculty. He remembered screwing a handful of other girls on campus, both while a student and afterwards; he just couldn't remember their names now. Hoss slipped out the front door.

Mrs. Krell recalled her detention, served the Monday after Prom for necking with Herby Spencer. She, too, slipped out the front door.

Mrs. Cassell remembered getting caught by Sister Mary Monica for carving "I Love Alfred" into her school desk in seventh grade. She followed Mrs. Krell.

Mr. Dangler thought of the time he had left a turd on the fifty-yard line late one Sunday night. He had not been caught, but what if someone had seen him and came forward with the damning revelation that it was he who left the gift on the field. What if they had more than visual evidence? What if they could prove that it was he who did the deed? What if they could produce the guano? How fast did shit decompose? Mr. Dangler turned redder and redder thinking of the shame his shit and consequent expulsion would bring on him and his family. He moved toward the front door faster than most.

Finally, only Mrs. Pruitt remained, pen in hand, ready to doom Christine Haverkamp, when suddenly a horrifying memory leapt into her mind. She recalled sitting in Sister Mary John's fourth grade classroom. While Sister was reading to them from *Tom Sawyer,* she, Thelma Pruitt, stared dreamily at Wilbur Schneiderjohn. Sister Mary John noticed this, stopped reading, and asked Thelma in front of the entire class: "Thelma, do you know what a newborn baby is like?"

Thelma nervously shook her head and squeaked, "No, Sister."

"You probably think they're cute and cuddly. They are…once they turn one. That first year, however, they are anything but cute and cuddly. They squirm and scream. They wake up every hour during the night. They need their diapers changed twenty to thirty times a day, and they leave fecal residue on their crib sheets that you, Thelma, have to wash with soap and your bare hands. They eat everything, *everything* that comes in sight—crumbs, cat hair, broken glass. And you have to constantly watch them or they could die on your watch and you're forever labeled a baby-killer. Do you know what sleep deprivation is? It was used by the Japanese to break American soldiers and force them to reveal top-secret information. Your baby will use the same tactics on you. Do you know where such little monsters come from, Thelma? They come into little ladies who stare too lustfully at little gentlemen! I suggest, Thelma, that you pay attention to Tom Sawyer and not Wilbur Schneiderjohn."

This sudden recollection turned Mrs. Pruitt red, and then white. What if the soon-to-be-established committee resurrected this unpleasant incident? And she a married woman? What would her husband think knowing that she had been unfaithful to him? Mrs. Pruitt let her pen fall to the ground, and she scuttled out of the school as quickly as she could.

Dr. Marquez went back into his office and asked Christine to peek into the hallway. She did and came back.

"Well," he said, "is anyone left demanding your expulsion?"

"No, sir," Christine replied meekly.

"Then that's that. I'm not going to expel you either. In fact, you'll have all the support I can give you. You've made a very brave decision in keeping this child. If you need anything, please let me know, and we'll do our best to balance your school schedule with your doctor visits."

An incredible feeling of relief and gratitude poured over Christine, and she rushed over to Dr. Marquez and hugged him with all her might.

Chapter 19

Spring Break had come at just the right time. Dr. Marquez was as outwardly enthusiastic and upbeat as ever, but the constant harassment from the Righteous Right was wearing on him. The school was slowly but surely emerging from decades of mismanagement and abuse. Enrollment was up. He was adored by the students and most of the community. Yet a number of his associations had begun to raise questions. Although the Buffalo Wild Wings dinner with Raul had initially blown over, the controversy was renewed when the two were seen eating together at a Chick-fil-A about a month later. Raul had found a job in Dallas and wished to thank Dr. Marquez for all his help, and to ask him to continue to look in now and then on his mother.

Later, Dr. Marquez was seen eating locally at Schmidt's with Karl Fritcher, who just five years previous had been released from prison after serving a five-year stint for possession of methamphetamine. Karl had stayed clean during those five years, but the collective memory of Wilhelmsburg stretched back far more than five years.

Just before the break, again at Schmidt's, Dr. Marquez was seen dining with Terry, his alcoholic neighbor. Terry's attempt at rehab was not as successful as Karl's time in jail. For five days, Terry was sober and high on life. Next weekend, he was drinking again. To his credit, his consumption had been cut in half, but that still meant he consumed a fifth or two a week.

These three associations, coupled with his continued friendship with various Wilhelmsburg ne'er-do-wells, damaged his reputation in the eyes of the town's self-appointed spiritual guardians.

Now, enjoying his first day of Spring Break, at least as much as the students were, Dr. Marquez was awaiting his usual Friday dinner at Schmidt's. He had ordered two chicken-fried chickens with sides of mashed potatoes, green beans, and corn. Additionally, he had placed an order for fried pickles and another for fried tomatoes. He planned to cap off the meal with a slice of carrot cake, thinking it healthier than the German chocolate cake. Afterwards, he would go home, sit on his back porch, and enjoy a half shot of Bacardi 151 in his coke and a nice cigar.

As he awaited his feast, Miss Leah Connell entered the restaurant. Miss Connell was more than moderately pretty, which explained how she came to have five different boyfriends, all since December. She currently lived with Greg Koesler, one of the local mechanics who worked in a shop in nearby Jefferson City. Miss Connell had a charming personality, adequate brains, and could be seen each Sunday at the 8:00 Mass. Still, she had had five boyfriends since Christmas and lived with a man out of wedlock.

Miss Connell walked straight toward the bar. Along the way, she looked down and noticed her shoe was untied. She stopped, bent her knee while raising her foot and placed it on an unoccupied chair in front of her. It was the chair next to Dr. Marquez. Shocked, Dr. Marquez looked over to say "hi" but failed to make eye contact as Miss Connell was focused on tying her shoestring. She had on a bright and pretty floral skirt which came down nearly to her knees. That is, it came nearly to her knees when she was standing up. With one leg raised more than two feet off the ground and her foot resting on top of a chair, the skirt revealed a little more. When he looked over to say "hi," Dr. Marquez's peripheral sight noticed an ivory thigh that was both toned and meaty, as well as a flash of bright red cloth that was either a thong or close kin to a thong. He immediately raised his head to look out the front door that Miss Connell had just pirouetted through, but now his peripheral vision caught sight of her chest that had been exposed as she bent over to reach her shoes. Her breasts, though not large, were firm and now larger than normal due to gravity. Dr. Marquez raised his eyes to read a poster along the wall above the front door. Now his peripheral vision soaked in the safety of the top of her brown hair. He looked up no further.

The inadvertent vision of her thigh, red cloth, and chest lasted the briefest of all brief moments. Yet, it burned in his mind. "Tempt not my weak eyes too often with sights like that, O Lord!" he thought to himself. He knew most of the guys in the bar envied his view. Those who could were straining their neck muscles and eyeballs in his direction, hoping the other shoe needed tying as well. He knew Mr. Ferro was three tables behind him, so at least one person in the bar was leaning over picking up a napkin or fork or morsel of food he had accidentally dropped on the ground so as to see around the immense bulk of the principal. He knew other men were cursing him for the broad shoulders and massive physique that blocked their own view. He also knew that all the women in the bar were looking in his direction, too. Not to see Miss Connell's cleavage, but to see if he was seeing Miss Connell's cleavage.

With half his mind, Dr. Marquez cursed the awkward situation he had unwillingly been placed in, while the other half laughed at the hilarious absurdity of it. He was at a table with a gorgeous young woman, and all eyes were on him! What he did in the next five seconds would either spark or defuse the next Wilhelmsburg controversy.

When Miss Connell finally secured her laces, she sprightly placed her foot on the ground and began pushing the chair in. She looked up and noticed with slight surprise Dr. Marquez sitting there. She did not notice the other thirty-two pairs of eyes on her.

"Good evening, Miss Connell."

"Oh…hello, I didn't notice you there. I'm sorry. My shoe came untied."

"That's quite alright. I'm just waiting on my food. I think they're making me digest my earlier meal before they bring me another. How are you? I hear your mother won Wilhelmsburg's 'Yard of the Month' award. And you? I understand you're just about to finish your lab tech certification?"

Miss Connell was used to young, unmarried men in Wilhelmsburg speaking with her, but older, married men and all women shunned her. Therefore, she was surprised to not only be spoken to in a polite manner by a leading citizen, especially in public, but to have another interested in her, her goals, and even her family.

"I am. I mean, I finish my program in two months."

"Oh, congratulations, then! You must be excited. My sister has been working in a lab for the last seven years and loves it. It's a great career you've chosen."

Meanwhile, all ears in the bar were straining with the same exertion as their owner's eyes to hear the conversation between Dr. Marquez and Leah Connell. An immense powder keg of a year's worth of gossip and scandal sat immobile while a bright flame with red undergarments was flickering dangerously near.

"And how's Todd? Or is your beau named Tom?" Dr. Marquez queried.

"Well, it was Todd. But now I'm seeing Greg."

"Greg Koesler?"

"Yep. That's him!" Leah beamed.

"Greg's working down at the shop in Jefferson City, isn't he?"

"Yep. I stay with him most of the time, but I try to get back to Wilhelmsburg on the weekend."

Dr. Marquez was disappointed but refused to show it. Leah was always bouncing around from the house of one suitor to another. Or rather, from one user to another. His heart ached for her, and a profound sense of pity caused him to say, "You know, Leah, you're about to have a really good job. You'll be doing something society needs and will get well compensated for it. Why don't you make an honest man out of one of your beaus?"

"Oh, Greg's going to marry me!" she exclaimed. "Just as soon as I finish my degree, and he gets the promotion he's in line for."

"Yes, I heard he might make foreman. That's a significant step up."

"Um hmm! I'm so proud of him."

"*Then* he's going to marry you?"

"Yep. He's already said so."

"Leah, I'm going to be frank with you. I think you're a fantastic woman. You got a lot going for you. But let me tell you how most men operate. Greg's going to live with you and get what he wants. And when he gets his promotion, he'll think you're holding him back, and he'll start looking for someone who is at his level financially. And, in the meantime, what if you end up with child?"

Leah started to object, but Dr. Marquez continued, "I know it's painful, and maybe I'm wrong about Greg, or a large number of other young men, but I've seen your situation played out so many times before. It almost always ends with the girl living with her boyfriend until he gets financially stable, and then it's the guy who moves on."

They both sat in silence for some moments. Then Dr. Marquez added, "I'm not trying to meddle in your business, Leah, but I just want to warn you about the mentality of a lot of men I know. I just don't want to see you taken advantage of. Now that you're so close to finishing your impressive degree. Just think about what I've said, will you?" He smiled at her. It was a smile that neither Greg nor any of her other boyfriends had ever given her. It was a deep smile, a smile directed at Leah the person, not Leah the body. She thanked Dr. Marquez and walked away from the table promising him she would think, really think, about what he had said.

Chapter 20

Dr. Marquez sat on his back porch enjoying the last Sunday of Spring Break. He was anxious to get back to his work at Holy Family. That is, his official 7:00-4:30 work. In effect, he had worked throughout the break as he worked throughout all breaks. But it was different when school was in session. There was no replacing the bustling halls, the teachers flitting to and fro, the continual flow of parents in and out of his office. He looked forward to the visitors, the excitement, the accomplishments, and the problems. Especially the problems. Dr. Marquez was uniquely suited for his job as principal. He gloried in the challenge and relished the everyday absurdities when dealing with his fellow men. In fact, it was his ability to laugh and find humor in seemingly serious, and sometimes tragic, situations that made him such a successful leader.

Dr. Marquez had just finished reading an article from Wilhelmsburg's weekly that he felt exemplified the town and all its hysterical eccentricities. The article was a clarion call to the pious of the community to boycott Wilhelmsburg's most popular and financially successful weekend: Germanfest. The event had raised a plethora of money for the town each year for the past thirty-four years. It included a variety of entertainment: shopping at more than a hundred vendor stands, more than a score of food and beer trucks, carnival rides for children, and a handful of live bands. This year, the Wilhelmsburg Chamber of Commerce had decided to include a Led Zeppelin tribute band as the festival's chief attraction.

Most citizens of Wilhelmsburg were thrilled and waited impatiently for the festival to arrive. However, the inevitable few feared and loathed the presence of a rock-and-roll band in town, especially a band known for its drug use. The most visible form of outrage appeared as a Letter to the Editor in the paper Dr. Marquez was reading.

I call upon the good citizens of Wilhelmsburg to join with me in resisting the invasion of a Led Zeppelin Tribute band that is scheduled to play at our local Germanfest. Wilhelmsburg is a good, quiet, Catholic town. Many of our citizens have moved here to escape the corrupting influences of society. They came here to raise their children far from the devilish noise of bands like Led Zeppelin. I would think our community could find another band more worthy of tribute.

For those of you who do not know, Led Zeppelin is a band that became popular in the 1960s, that era of Satan, drugs, and decadence. Therefore, its songs pay homage to the demons that inspire them. For example, if you spell their hit song *Stairway to Heaven* backwards, it spells *Nevaeh ot Yawriats*. That's right, its gibberish—the language spoken at Babel. Do we want our children singing songs in the language of Nimrod? Furthermore, if you play any of Led Zeppelin's songs backwards, you will see that the lyrics are tributes to Satan himself. And we want to pay this band to sing such devil music to our children!!!

Now, when my petition goes through and this band is cast back into the Gehenna from which it sprang, there will be a void in the music venue. I understand that once we rid ourselves of the eleventh plague that is Led Zeppelin, we will also drive out the remaining rock bands, creating an even greater void. Not to worry, I have a plan. I propose to you that our church's children's choir fill that void. Of course, we will have three empty stages and twelve hours a day, Thursday through Sunday to fill, but this is where the beauty of my plan shows itself. Our young children will fill *all* the empty slots. We all know idle hands do the devil's work. So, we will ensure that idleness not be an option for our young ones. We will shuffle them from stage to stage and song to song and their sweet, melodious voices will sing the praises of God all weekend long. Our children thereby will not only be protected from satanic cult bands, but will also learn the virtue of hard work. What about their meals you ask? Well, doesn't the Bible tell us that great good comes from prayer and fasting? And, if singing is praying twice, and our children are singing, why not have them offer a twelve-hour fast as well? What could be more pleasing to our Lord than singing, fasting children?

Signed,
A Concerned and Very Holy Catholic

Dr. Marquez re-read the letter for the third time and laughed just as boisterously then as he had the first time. "God, how I love this community," he thought.

Chapter 21

The beginning of the end began during senior high lunch. Herman Knorr sat with his senior friends and scanned the freshman table for a likely victim. He zoned in on the face of Caitlyn Brashear. The giddiest of freshmen girls, Caitlyn provided the most likely target as she would spend half the lunch period with her mouth wide open, talking or laughing.

Herman elbowed the two guys next to him, set his cafeteria-hardened pinto bean on the table, and took aim. It took Caitlyn about ten seconds before she began laughing, mouth agape. But not agape enough. Herman bided his time, waiting for Caitlyn to break into extended and raucous laughter. He didn't have to wait long. Soon she was laughing again, and her mouth was as wide as needed for a can't-miss shot. He elbowed his classmates again to get their attention. Braden Grewing looked up and advised, "Wait, you'll get a clearer shot later." Dalton Jackson added, "Yeah, man, don't fire 'til you see the red of her tonsils." Herman ignored the advice, trusting in his own skill as a hardened bean shooter. He pulled the first knuckle of his right middle finger and tucked it into the soft underside of his thumb knuckle. He aimed, he fired, he missed.

Herman had had extensive experience flicking various objects across crowded rooms at inappropriate times. He generally found his mark, whether it be with a paperclip, small rock, pen top, the ever-trustworthy spitball, and on occasion, even bubble gum. The ability to flick the latter and not have it stick to his hand, and sometimes to flick it accurately, too, had made Herman's stock rise in his classmates' eyes ever since he unveiled this unique and potent skill as a kindergartener.

Today's launch, however, resembled the Project Vanguard launch failure. Herman was a prankster, and a good one at that, but he was no Booth or Oswald. The dried bean never arched. Instead, it maintained its trajectory up until the moment it hit Caitlyn just above her right eye. She screamed, the seniors softly giggled, and the rest of the cafeteria looked in Caitlyn's direction in expectant silence. Alex Hanssen, a freshmen known more for his choir skills than football prowess—though he still played as was expected of any Holy Family male—dropped his tray on the ground, breaking the silence. Instead of the usual clapping, everyone turned to Alex and screamed with their eyes, "Shut up!" and then looked back to Caitlyn, some in genuine concern, some in morbid curiosity, others hoping to see a fight, pints of oozing blood, or at least an eyeball rolling along the floor. Instead, they saw Caitlyn holding her eye and sobbing.

Presently, Dr. Marquez walked into the cafeteria minutes behind Mr. Ferro and Ms. Briton. At first, he noticed the silence. And then the sobbing. He looked in that direction and saw it was Caitlyn Brashear. He instantly deduced two possibilities: she was either sobbing in pain or crying at the hilarity of one of her own jokes, as she had been known to do on occasion. The noise coming from Caitlyn, coupled with the crowd's silence, convinced him it was a pain-moan.

He and Ms. Briton walked toward Caitlyn. Mr. Ferro fell behind two steps so as to get a better view of one of their backsides; only Dr. Marquez knew whose. With her arm on Caitlyn's shoulder, Ms. Briton leaned over to ask her why she wept. Dr. Marquez stood by and listened for the explanation, and Mr. Ferro stood not listening at all, but looking intently.

Dr. Marquez could make out only a little as to what happened between Caitlyn's sobs. It was the burnt bean on the table that revealed to him the secondary cause of what had now become an intense wailing. The lowered eyes of the senior boys, focused on eating their lunch in peace, while all other eyes looked alternatively from Caitlyn to himself, revealed to him the primary cause.

"All right. I'll handle this. Mrs. Britton, why don't you eat your lunch? I'll walk Miss Brashear over to the school nurse."

"Oh, I don't mind helping her, Dr. Marquez."

"I know, but you've got a class in thirty, now twenty-five minutes. Eat your food. I can always have the good ladies of the cafeteria send a boxed lunch over to my office. Besides, a little fasting won't do me any harm. I've got enough reserves to last me until the end of the school year."

Dr. Marquez laughed at himself loudly. Mrs. Britton laughed less loudly in polite accompaniment and returned to her table with Mr. Ferro behind, at a safe enough distance where he could casually lower his eyes toward the floor, catching a glimpse of something else on the way down. All eyes had been turned towards the teary cheeks of Caitlyn Brashear. Mr. Ferro's eyes had been turned toward a different set of cheeks.

Three hundred yards, round trip, and half a dozen jokes later, Dr. Marquez was on his way back to the cafeteria. All he learned from Caitlyn was that a projectile of either immense size or lightening velocity, or perhaps both, had struck her in the eye. She suggested it might have been a BB, buckshot, or perhaps an arrowhead that presently threatened her with a detached retina at best, permanent blindness at worst. Dr. Marquez noticed a red splotch on her temple, just above her right eyebrow. Convinced that it probably had not penetrated far enough into her skull to cause permanent, or even temporary, eye damage, Dr. Marquez got Caitlyn to the nurse, suggested an ice pack, and had the secretary phone Caitlyn's mother.

On the way back to the cafeteria, he had thought of how to handle this situation. He knew who the culprits were; now he had to figure out how to deal with them. The projectile clearly came from the Senior boys, but which one? He determined to figure out who and then let the punishment fall on him.

Unfortunately for Dr. Marquez, although he did suspect it would be the case, none of the boys claimed responsibility. He decided to let the high school finish lunch and then held the particular table in question. Again, he asked who the culprit was. Again, no one claimed responsibility. Clearly, this was not Al-Quaeda or the IRA he was dealing with, but a far more clandestine organization. He decided on a different approach. He stepped outside the cafeteria and interrogated the boys one by one, again with no tangible results—they all professed ignorance.

Dr. Marquez briefly considered attempting Taliban-style interrogating techniques. He would slap each boy as he came to him twice on the side of the head before questioning him. Surely, this would accomplish two objectives: he would gather the sought after information, and his slap, with an open palm, could not be considered torture, thereby assuring that he would not be in violation of the Geneva Convention. He gave serious thought to proceeding thusly. Only the remembrance of twenty-first century American legal customs and an overly litigious culture stayed his hand…and the realization that a slap from his gargantuan paws, with nearly four hundred pounds of pressure behind them, might do more damage to eighteen-year-old skulls than would a slap from a much more diminutive Afghan.

Dr. Marquez was not easily rattled, and he wasn't now. But he was running out of options. He played his last card and told the boys that they were their brother's keeper and all would be punished if someone did not come forth with the identity of the culprit before 3:30. He was met with a combination of icy stares and downcast looks. He returned to his office to await the outcome of his threat.

At 3:45, Dr. Marquez phoned Coach Koch and let him know that nine Senior boys, the entire Senior football class, would not be suiting up for Spring practice, even though a scrimmage had already been planned for the upcoming Friday. They were all receiving a week's worth of detentions which would prohibit them from extra-curricular activities, including football practice and games.

Before four o'clock, Dr. Marquez had three angry parents in his office. By four fifteen, the number had grown to nine, the parents of all the boys who had been detentioned. By four thirty, fifteen incensed parents awaited his explanation. By five fifteen, more than forty.

Unwittingly, Dr. Marquez had opened Pandora's box, crossed the River Styx, encountered Minos, forded the Rubicon, and broke the kettles and sunk the boats. By long experience, he knew he had made the right decision, but he also knew he had desecrated the Holy Grail, the Ark of the Covenant, the Kaaba, the sacred beard of Zeus: Mississippi high school football. The two sides were rapidly approaching Armageddon, and it would take place not on Patmos or the Holy Land, but in the principal's office at Holy Family in Wilhelmsburg, Mississippi.

Chapter 22

The meeting the night before had not been a pleasant one. The supporters of Holy Family football had wanted to take Dr. Marquez to the top of Schmidt's and hurl him off. Had they been able to lift and maneuver him to the roof top, they might have done just that. However, when ten p.m. rolled around, Dr. Marquez passed harmlessly through the midst of them.

But his fate was sealed.

The next morning, he entered the school building after directing the drop-off line and making sure everything was in order for the morning's Mass. He made his way to his office, waddled in, and fired up his computer. As he waited to log on, he noticed a piece of paper on his desk. It was a ninety-five word ultimatum demanding that he allow the Senior boys to participate in Friday night's game. Should he refuse to do so, his position as principal would be reevaluated immediately. Dr. Marquez recognized a serious threat when he saw one. The first e-mail he read, and the second, and the third, and the thirty-third, confirmed this threat.

He sat back and reflected. He wanted desperately to remain at Holy Family, but he knew the odds were against him. The presence of Hoss at the impromptu meeting to expel Christine Haverkamp had alerted Dr. Marquez to an unpleasant change in the wind. For the first time since he had arrived in Wilhelmsburg, a football fanatic had cast his die with the holy rollers. If the holy rollers presently threw their weight behind the fanatics, he knew he would be looking for another job, for he also knew that in good conscious he couldn't give in to either side.

He began to shift in his double wide chair, his backend beginning to burn with the heat of the seat. He decided to call a few of his friends and enjoy a good brunch at Schmidt's before he made his decision.

Chapter 23

Mr. Ferro, Terry, and Dr. Marquez sat at Schmidt's eating scrambled eggs with bacon, a ham and cheese omelet with a red draw, and eggs with bacon along with a ham and cheese omelet, respectively. Dr. Marquez had hoped to dine with Mr. Meyer as well, but he couldn't get hold of him. This was unusual because Mr. Meyer was always messing with his phone. Dr. Marquez refused to entertain the thought that Mr. Meyer was avoiding him at this unpleasant time.

"Well, boys, it looks as if I've built my own coffin."

Mr. Ferro and Terry knew exactly what he was talking about, but both feigned ignorance. Terry said, "That so, Doc? What'd you do this time?"

Mr. Ferro was looking down at his plate chopping up his already scrambled eggs.

Dr. Marquez gave an account of the flight of the burned bean, the near fatality, and the suspension of football-related activities.

"Shiiiit. Tough spot, Doc. I dunno know how you're gonna get out of this one," replied Terry.

"Seems to me that you're up shit creek without a paddle."

Mr. Ferro said nothing and continued to take smaller and smaller bites out of his diminishing pile of eggs, hoping they would last until the conversation changed.

"Well, gentlemen, I enjoyed breakfast, but I better get back to work and sort all this out. Thanks for showing up, and I'll catch up with ya'll later." Dr. Marquez paid his bill, leaving a generous tip and walked toward the front door. He nodded at a few of the Holy Family parents as he left Schmidt's. They didn't nod back.

Chapter 24

Dr. Marquez knew the hour of reckoning was at hand. Instead of going back to his office, he decided to spend some time in reflection with Father Pat. He drove by the cemetery and parked at the rectory. He was hoping to share some of his stress and anxiety with the priest.

Father Pat was not watering his plants as he normally did on Saturday mornings. Dr. Marquez sat in his car gathering his thoughts, trying to figure out an acceptable solution to the maelstrom brewing around him.

He called Mr. Meyer again. No answer.

He went back to seeking the elusive solution.

He called Ms. Yerma, to remind her that it was only the nine Senior boys who would not be playing Friday night, but that the punishment did not extend to the Senior cheerleaders. He was also hoping for a sympathetic ear. Ms. Yerma was the school's disciplinarian, and surely she would side with him. No answer.

He went back to his increasingly mournful catch-22. He didn't want to alienate the school community and likely lose his job. He wished now that Holy Family had had a dean of students to handle this issue. He wanted desperately to pass the bitter cup of leadership on to someone else. He briefly thought of leaving the punishment up to Mr. Ferro and Ms. Briton, the two teachers on cafeteria duty that day. He even thought of placing his responsibility on Father Pat.

He finally got out of his car and made his way slowly up the rectory steps and rang the doorbell. No answer.

Dr. Marquez felt utterly alone and abandoned. He realized that he could simply walk away. Not permanently, but for a three-, or perhaps four-day weekend. He never took days off. He could even call in sick and have Coach Koch fill in for him. That way, he could save face, the boys would play in Friday night's game, and the situation would blow over. It really was very simple.

Yet Dr. Marquez realized that simple was not, in this case, right.

He sighed deeply, restarted his engine, and began to back down the driveway, unable to shake his feeling of abandonment. He drove down Main Street and glanced down the side street where Holy Family stood. He saw more than two dozen cars parked in front of the main office. He kept driving.

Chapter 25

Dr. Marquez continued down Main Street and glanced over towards his house on Second Street. It, too, had a handful of cars parked in front. He understood and accepted that a confrontation he was doomed to lose was now inevitable. Too many people had become too emotionally invested in the punishment he had doled out. They would be satisfied with nothing less than a complete retraction or a resignation.

He pulled into the parking lot across from Schmidt's to gather his thoughts before going to face the wrath that awaited him at his office.

He had already resolved to confront this crisis head-on. To him, it was a matter of priorities. It was a decision that would punish young men and almost certainly cost their football teammates a game. The alternative was to enable them to play and thereby reinforce the notion that sports came first; that there were no consequences for varsity players; that mom and dad will always be there to bail them out.

Dr. Marquez's thoughts were racing, and his subconscious was working overtime. Finally, his mind focused on a book he had just finished, *The Bridge at Andau* by James Michener.

Michener spoke of the God-like love of parents living in communist-occupied Hungary. Many parents felt it their duty to expose their children to the doctrines of the free world. Therefore, they taught them the principles of subjectivity, solidarity, personal responsibility, free will, and a number of other virtues associated with freedom and religion. A number of these same parents took it a step further and educated their children in the faith, both Catholic and Protestant. Such an education was an act of near *agape* love, for inevitably, children being children, would at times need to be disciplined. When such a day came, the parent was faced with an agonizing decision. If he spanked and punished his child, the child, again, being a child with his concomitant naivety, just might go to the teacher and exact his revenge and tell the teacher what he had been taught at home. Later that night, the parent could expect a visit from the state police and a train ride from which he would never return. The alternative was to overlook the child's misdeeds. And the next infraction. And the next. And soon the parent becomes the guardian of a sorry creature unfit to take his ranks amongst the world's free men, and even more importantly, unprepared for the Final Judgment. Thus, the Hungarian parents of the 1940s and '50s demonstrated superhuman love each and every time they took the belt to their wayward children. Yet, as Dr. Marquez reflected, it was those children, the ones who had been disciplined, who would later lead their nation in the fight to overthrow their Soviet oppressors, for they had learned the meaning of sacrifice and love when it was so very dangerous to love.

Dr. Marquez decided once and for all to act the parent the senior parents chose not to be.

He decided to call Mr. Meyer again. Again, no answer. He called Ms. Yerma. Straight to voicemail. He was about to call Mr. Ferro when he saw Terry approaching his car. Terry's head was down. Dr. Marquez finally caught his eye when he shouted as jubilantly as ever, "Terry, my friend, long time no see!" He laughed, even when he saw the pained look on Terry's face. Only then did Dr. Marquez notice Roger Wagner, Daniel Wolf, and Mrs. Pruitt in the distance behind him. So, this is how it would end.

Terry extended his hand and offered it to Dr. Marquez saying, "Doc, you got a few minutes? I'd like to speak with you a minute."

Dr. Marquez shook his hand and said, still smiling, "Sure, Terry. What's on your mind?" Although he was thinking, "Terry, you Cassius! You Brutus! You Hagan! You Judas! You betray me with a handshake?!" And then he looked again into Terry's pained eyes, and he was no longer angry with him; he was filled with a deep sense of pity for the wretch that stood before him reeking of booze. The red draws at Schmidt's earlier that morning had not made him smell so. No, the whiskey odor came from a bottle bought at the liquor store, most likely bought by the three persons watching Terry betray his friend. They had promised Terry something and then sealed the deal with some shots. Dr. Marquez tried hard to dismiss these uncharitable thoughts, but he knew truth when it presented itself to him. He also knew human nature. Terry would so regret his betrayal that he would immediately go on a dangerous bender, perhaps his last. Dr. Marquez gave Terry a hug and told him to head on home; they would talk tomorrow. Besides, he had an appointment at his office in five minutes. Grateful to be given an excuse to avoid the scene about to unfold, Terry headed back to his truck. He drove straight home, grabbed the two fifths of whiskey on the passenger seat and headed inside.

Chapter 26

Dr. Marquez started his engine and began to drive back up Main Street towards Sixth where he would at last confront his doom. Two minutes later, he was parking his car in front of the school. The mob was anxiously awaiting, having been texted by Daniel Wolf and informed that Terry had fulfilled his end of the bargain. Dr. Marquez, however, decided to make them wait. His phone had buzzed when he was talking to Terry, and he figured now would be a good time to check his voicemail. He did. It was Mr. Ferro who informed him that he had decided to sign a contract back at his alma mater in Macon, Georgia. Mr. Ferro explained that it would put him closer to his family and fiancé in Georgia. Dr. Marquez understood that the pressure of the holy rollers had broken Mr. Ferro. With his favorite, and most popular, teacher gone, Dr. Marquez now prepared to face his Inquisition without a single ally in the school.

Chapter 27

For the first time in his life, Dr. Marquez held his tongue in a crowded room. He sat in the library where the meeting would be held, in silence. The questioning, criticism, and abuse came from all directions. And he answered all the assaults the same, with silence.

Exasperated, Mrs. Pruitt, who had not attended a single Holy Family football game in three years on account of the ungodly cheerleader uniforms that bore neither crucifixes nor fish nor *chi rhos*, but terminated in flesh just six inches below the hipbone, but who had finally found a cause to drive out the principal who refused to enforce her brand of Catholicism, stood and asked Dr. Marquez point blank: "Tell us, Dr. Marquez, are you going to let our good Catholic boys play next Friday or not?"

Dr. Marquez replied, "You know I cannot do that, Mrs. Pruitt. The suspension stands."

The library filled with a shriek that could have been a martyr being burned or an apostate angel falling to the fires of hell after his rebellion. Everyone looked toward the source of the wail and saw Mrs.

Pruitt standing up and tearing asunder the scarf that many had thought to be permanently attached to her head, having never seen her without it. She looked wildly around her and screeched, "You have heard it from his own mouth! How can we work with a man so stubborn, so vile, so mean-spirited? How can this man lead our school? How can we trust him with our children?"

The library filled with shouts, condemnations, and applause. Mrs. Pruitt raised her voice above the den and shouted, "What is your decision? What do we do with Dr. Marquez?"

"Fire him! Fire him!" was resonating throughout the library when Roger Wagner, a member of the school board as well as wealthy benefactor, quieted the room and reminded the mob, "The decision is made. We'll get ourselves a new principal. One who will respect our ways and our children. But we have no authority to fire and hire principals. We need the school board's permission."

Chants of "Today! Today! Right now!" filled the room. Dr. Marquez, not wanting to delay the decision that would determine his future, agreed to accompany the mob to the house of Father Pat.

In order to officially fire Dr. Marquez, the mob would need the approval of four of seven board members. Terry had already cast his vote *in abstentia*. With Roger Wagner acting as co-ringleader, along with Mrs. Pruitt, during the gathering in the library, his vote to terminate Dr. Marquez's contract was assured. If Fr. Pat came on board, there would be no need to visit Linda Muller, as the anti-Marquez faction would have the necessary votes.

The procession to Fr. Pat's began. Dr. Marquez's every step was a chore. Besides the stress it put on his immense physique, he was simply beat down emotionally. The mob, Terry, Mr. Ferro, it was almost too much to take in all at once.

They finally arrived at the rectory, and this time Fr. Pat answered his door. Seeing Dr. Marquez flanked by Mrs. Pruitt and Roger Wagner, and they in turn backed by an immense mob, he quickly surmised the situation. Mrs. Pruitt and Roger Wagner just as quickly confirmed his suspicions and fears: Dr. Marquez stood on trial for his principalship.

The complaints rolled off the tongues of the recently self-deputized constables. Fr. Pat knew the charges; he had heard them many times before. Principals simply didn't last long at Holy Family. Those that did threw their weight behind either the holy rollers or the football team and played one against the other. Yet, Dr. Marquez seemed to have alienated both. In fact, the two rival factions had set aside their differences, at least until the demise of Dr. Marquez, and had joined forces against a perceived greater threat. "Well done, Frank" thought Fr. Pat. He longed to tell Dr. Marquez, "To be like Christ, you gotta piss some people off, and if you're not pissing someone off, you're not doing your job, but you, Frank, seemed to have pissed everyone off." Instead, Fr. Pat simply listened to the litany of charges against the unfortunate principal.

Finally, the accusations ended, and Fr. Pat looked at Dr. Marquez and said, "You seemed to have aroused quite a bit of animosity here. Do you think there is any way this unfortunate situation can be worked out? Maybe some sort of compromise is in store?"

Dr. Marquez looked up at Fr. Pat and then lowered his head and shook it slowly from side to side.

"That's it? Come on, Frank! You got to give me something," thought Fr. Pat. He said, "You look like a distraught fourth grader, Frank. Are you sure your decision is final?"

This time, Dr. Marquez shook his head positively.

Fr. Pat reprimanded Dr. Marquez in his mind: "Son of a gun, Frank! *Now* you clam up. Of all times to shut your garrulous mouth! Give me something. I'm on your side, but you got to help me out. Don't you want this position you've given so much to these last nine months?"

"Do you have anything to say, Frank? Any defense?"

Silence.

A gut-pain filled Fr. Pat's core. He was furious at being placed in this position, and furious at Dr. Marquez for not defending himself. The mob began to murmur louder and louder, and he knew he owed them a decision. He proclaimed from the rectory steps: "I believe Dr Marquez has good intentions, and that he has done a lot of good for our school. I strongly believe we should give him a chance." The murmurs became stunned and bitter invectives. "But if he will not compromise, I don't see how we can solve this dilemma." Fr. Pat understood that if he backed Dr. Marquez unconditionally, parents would begin to systematically withdraw their children from Holy Family. The school community as a whole would be harmed, and all because of Dr. Marquez's refusal to compromise. "Therefore, I advise the members of the School Board to settle this yourselves. It's my strong hope that you reach a compromise, but I'll back the Board in whatever they decide."

Dr. Marquez had known what his fate would be all along, but now the finality of it struck him like a wrecking ball. He looked up to Fr. Pat, for he had been hoping that Fr. Pat would understand why he refused to compromise, but the priest had already turned his back on the mob and Dr. Marquez and headed toward the rectory door. Without turning around, he shut the door behind him. The clicking of the doorknob and the bolting of the lock from the inside drowned out the victorious cheers of the Inquisition. "To Linda's! To Linda's!" howled the delighted mob.

Chapter 28

The fit walked, the elders drove, but all arrived *en masse* at Linda Muller's house on First Street. Linda was used to sleeping in on Saturdays and was not too pleased at being awoken. Nevertheless, she answered the door. Seeing the crowd outside and the unmistakable figure of Dr. Marquez, she assumed he had again done something foolish. She had heard rumors of some varsity football players being suspended, but she knew that Dr. Marquez knew better.

She thought he knew better. Without exchanging pleasantries, Mrs. Pruitt got straight to the point. "So, it is true," thought Linda, "Why, Dr. Marquez? Surely you knew not to open up that can of worms?" Reluctantly, she invited the ringleaders, Mrs. Pruitt, Daniel, and Roger, into her home. The trio was not anxious to enter the Muller house. Linda was a mother of four, and her husband worked one week on and one week off on an oil rig. He was working this week, and the four little ones knew it. As soon as they awoke, the Muller house would operate in imitation of hell's second circle. It would not be Paolo, Francesca, Tristan, and Isolde that turned the Muller home into a tornado of activity, but Justin, Zane, Dale, and Danielle. Mrs. Pruitt suspected that the children had been spawned not by Mr. Muller, but by Minos himself.

When Mrs. Pruitt, her son-in-law, and Roger refused to enter, Linda asked to speak with Dr. Marquez, alone. Although she wanted to control the proceedings, Mrs. Pruitt justified releasing her prisoner by telling herself that putting up with the Muller children was a good preliminary punishment for Dr. Marquez.

As the mob waited outside, Dr. Marquez took a seat at the Muller table. As soon as he did so, the first two Muller children awoke and came bursting into the dining room. Linda immediately began rebuking them and telling them to return to their rooms for the time being; she would cook them breakfast later. Outside, the crowd heard the familiar sound of Dr. Marquez's uproarious laughter. Inside, Linda heard him say, "Oh, Linda, it's alright. One of life's greatest pleasures is the sound of kids laughing in the morning."

"But Dr. Marquez, we need to talk, and they're so loud."

"They're *alive*, Linda. Children should be active and curious. It's the sign of a large soul."

The two little ones ran up to Dr. Marquez and leapt unto his knee. He laughed loudly. They screeched all the louder, and so did he. Linda looked on and smiled. She knew what others said about her rambunctious children, and she appreciated Dr. Marquez's kind words, and she knew he meant them.

As much as Linda enjoyed seeing her children interact with an adult who enjoyed their vivacity, she knew the next ten minutes would not be pleasant. Her interrogation began.

"So, Dr. Marquez, could you not have left well enough alone?" she asked, with sorrowful, pleading eyes.

"This time…no, Linda, I could not. This is important. Not to me, but to the school and especially to those senior boys."

Linda lowered her head and nodded slowly. She knew Dr. Marquez was not going to back down on this issue. She also knew how this conversation was going to end and what would happen shortly thereafter. Nevertheless, she pleaded with him to change his mind, but to no avail. Sadly, she went outside and told the mob that she wasn't sure this particular issue was a fireable offense. To this, Mrs. Pruitt replied that her, Linda Muller's, time as Holy Family Board Member was limited, as school board elections would be held within the month. If she hoped for a sixth term, she had better acquiesce to the requests of the school community. And that request now was the removal of Dr. Marquez.

Flustered, Linda went back inside to speak again with Dr. Marquez. Five minutes later, she was outside. She proposed having Dr. Marquez reprimanded and stripped of his duties as dean of students' discipline. But it was too little too late. The mob had sniffed blood and would settle for nothing less than the ruin of Dr. Marquez. Dr. Marquez knew it, and so did Linda Muller. She went back inside and made another futile attempt to reason with the principal she had helped hire nine months ago. Predictably, the result was the same.

One last time, Linda tried to pacify the crowd outside her house. She almost begged them to reconsider, but Mrs. Pruitt again threatened her with the certainty of replacing her on the school board next election. In addition, Mrs. Pruitt explained that while she, Linda, dallied inside with Dr. Marquez, the mob had discussed the option of reporting Linda's uncooperativeness to both the bishop and the superintendent, both of whom Mrs. Pruitt claimed to be working on behalf of.

These threats and Dr. Marquez's refusal to defend himself made it clear to Linda that the game was over. She, Dr. Marquez, and Holy Family Catholic School had lost. She said, "I don't think we ought to replace Dr. Marquez….But it is clear it is the wish of the school community to do so. I won't stand in your way."

A loud cheer went up which Dr. Marquez heard inside the house. He lifted himself from his chair as quickly as his bulk would allow and made his way to the door. He got there just as Linda was walking back in to tell him the news. He saved her the shame by telling her that he already knew and that it was for the best. He smiled his usual jovial smile, patted her on the shoulder, and walked through her door for the last time.

Linda called her neighbor and asked her if she could send her children over for an hour or so. She quickly dressed her four children and hurried them next door. Linda then returned home, went upstairs, filled her tub with hot, soapy water, and tried to wash the morning's events away.

Chapter 29

Early that afternoon Terry showed up outside Mrs. Pruitt's house. It had been four hours since he had entered his house with two fifths of whiskey. Mrs. Pruitt raised the curtain on her window and looked out. She did not know how much of that whiskey matriculated down Terry's throat, but judging by the truck with two passenger wheels over the curb, quite a lot.

Terry took a few steps toward the house and stumbled. He lifted himself back up and hollered in a slurred voice, "Thelma! Get your ass out here! Now! You, too, Roger and Pat, er Fader Pat, or whatever you are, and any ov yer other sonova bitches!"

Thelma shut the blinds quickly, turned to the others, and said, "It's just Terry. He's drunk. Leave him be, and he'll go away."

Terry stopped several feet from the door and commenced his hollering. "You deceived me, you bitch! Get out here—I don't want your fuckin' whiskey. Frank's my friend. One of my only friends, and you tricked me into backstabbing him! You don't fire him. You hear me woman? You let that man keep his job. He's good for the school. He's good for all of us."

Terry's rage was met with only silence. No sound came from the house. Terry walked back to his truck and opened the passenger door. He came back to the house with a full, unopened fifth and the other fifth four-fifths drunk. He placed the full bottle on the doorstep and shouted, "Here's your blood likker back. I on't want it. Take your fuckin' whiskey and you leave Frank alone, ya hear?"

Terry stood there waiting. No one answered, and so he turned to leave. When he got nearly to his truck, he turned one last time towards Mrs. Pruitt's house. He caught her peeking at him from behind the curtain and then saw the curtain shut immediately. He lifted the last of his drink and hurled it at the front steps, shattering it all over the porch. He then ran to the driver's side and drove to the end of the street where he could drive no more due to the tears streaming down his face.

When they were sure Terry had driven off, Roger opened the door and stepped over the broken glass towards the unopened bottle. He lifted it and said, "Well we might as well celebrate. Two birds in one day. We offed the Doctor and now I have a feeling we won't have to put up with Terry anymore."

Roger was walking inside with the whiskey when Mrs. Pruitt snapped at him: "Don't bring that in here!"

"Why not?" Roger asked.

"First of all, I don't want that devil's brew in my house. Secondly, he's right—that is blood liquor. We got what we wanted, and we did what was necessary, but that liquor is a stain, and I won't have it in my house. Sell it to some bum in Monroe and we'll donate the proceeds to Holy Family's cemetery extension fund."

Chapter 30

The Guardians of Morality worked frantically over the next few hours preparing the paperwork that would officially remove Dr. Marquez from Holy Family. It was their intention to present the official documents to Fr. Pat first thing in the morning and then forward them on to the bishop and superintendent. Dr. Marquez himself would receive the documents just after the bishop was faxed.

With his firing imminent, Dr. Marquez sat in his office grading papers just as he did every Saturday afternoon. He was under no illusions as to his fate, but he was still, at the moment, principal, and a teacher. In addition, he had an ACT Prep class to teach that afternoon, and he planned to fulfill that obligation. After all, he was at Holy Family not for the likes of Mrs. Pruitt, but for the students.

When he heard talking and laughter coming from upstairs, he knew the students had arrived. Sighing, but eager to get to his students, he put his remaining papers down and picked up the wooden box that held his prep materials and began to make his way up to room 204. As he approached the stairs, he felt a bit dizzy and nearly stumbled. He reached his hand out just in time and grabbed the beginning of the guardrail and balanced himself. Half a minute later he was ascending the stairs again. Halfway up he felt himself dizzying again, and again he stopped to catch his breath. At that moment Hayden Haverkamp came running wildly down the stairs and nearly ran into Dr. Marquez. He noticed his principal—and ACT prep teacher—was sweating profusely. Concerned, Hayden stopped and asked Dr. Marquez if he needed any help. Dr. Marquez wheezed and said he was only out of breath; it must be the heavy breakfast he had eaten. Hayden picked up the handkerchief that had fallen out of Dr. Marquez's pocket and gave it to him so that Dr. Marquez could wipe his increasingly sweaty head. He also took hold of the wooden box of Prep materials and began walking toward room 204.

Dr. Marquez finally and ploddingly made his way into Room 204. He used a large store of his remaining energy to smile at his students. He tried to laugh, but didn't have the breath for it, and he began to choke. Some of the students realized that this was not simply fat man wheezing. Something was wrong. But Dr. Marquez simply sat down and smiled at them. He took in several deep breaths, and the class took their seats and began to relax.

Dr. Marquez heaved himself upwards and waddled to the lectern. Just as he was about to begin the lesson, he felt a sharp pain on the left side of his chest. His arm shot up and tried to grab the source of the pain. After a massive inhalation, he struggled to exhale, and the pain grew worse, and then unbear-able. And then he felt no more.

Epilogue

When he regained consciousness, Dr. Marquez was standing beneath an impossibly high barbed-wire fence, alone. Shortly, a person appeared on the other side. The two stood looking at one another timelessly. Then the other spoke. Or rather, Dr. Marquez perceived him speaking the word, "Come." Dr. Marquez looked at the barbed-wire towering above him and laughed to himself. How could his mighty bulk make the ascent? Nevertheless, he began to climb. The wire tore into his flesh. It ripped, gnarled, and sliced his body in places he hadn't seen in decades. The pain was excruciating, but he continued to climb. Why and how, he couldn't fathom, but continue to climb he did. He felt warm blood ooze all over his now naked body and icy steel pierce his insides. But still he climbed. Oddly, the higher he got, the easier the climb became. It was as if he grew lighter, nay, airier. Yet he dared not look down at his mangled flesh for fear of what he would see.

Finally, he reached the fence's apex. He gingerly and sprightly swung his bulk over and began to descend, painlessly and easily. He had never felt so light and free before, not even as a five-year-old-boy at recess in the Florida Keys. Suddenly, he was aware of the person standing in front of him, the person who had said, "Come." The two looked again at one another, and the man said "Look," and pointed toward the fence. Dr. Marquez did not want to look back and see his old self. He did not want to look back and see pieces of his own quivering flesh impaled by the icy steel. He did not want to look back at what he left behind, his true self, the self he was ashamed of. He had wanted to be so much more, to live so much longer, to accomplish so, so much. He hadn't done enough, and the thought of all his unfinished work, his deeds undone, his omissions caused him great grief.

With great embarrassment, he raised his eyes and saw the mysterious person still pointing behind him. With great reluctance and dread, Dr. Marquez turned and looked at the fence. In awe-filled astonishment, he noticed the fence was covered not in bloody bits of flesh. Where the flesh should have been lay impaled a strange substance that resembled cotton or wool or bread, and yet none of these. A breath of wind began to gently blow around Dr. Marquez and his laconic comrade, and the mystery flesh began to flutter, disengage itself from the fence and fall slowly and beautifully downward.

Dr. Marquez turned amazed and questioning eyes to his silent companion who finally spoke. He told the recently deceased principal that what he had left behind in the fence was his life's work, and now that work was being returned to earth. The two watched the milky white particles fall for a long, long time, for Dr. Marquez had left behind an enormity of deeds, and his actions affected untold numbers of people who had come to know him. The cottony substance fell on the Keys, on Puerto Rico, Los Angeles and scores of places in between. Sheet after sheet rained down upon Wilhelmsburg.

Finally, the guide spoke up again: "Your work is done, Francisco, and it was well done. Let the seeds of your life continue to fall. And fall they will for a long time yet. We must be on our way."

The two turned their backs to the fence and began a brisk walk to what looked to Dr. Marquez to be an endless wall, tall and beautiful beyond description. As they approached it, he finally asked his guide who he was. The man replied: "I'm your guide. Your patron, you might say I first walked with Tobias, now with you, and with many more yet to come." He looked over and smiled at Dr. Marquez who in a sudden, flashing insight knew the identity of this kind and mysterious person.

Dr. Marquez began to chuckle. The chuckle built into a laugh. Before the laugh became uncontainable, he stopped and asked his guide, "Was your first mission really to help a man get bird shit out of his eye?"

His guide began to chuckle, too, and replied affirmatively. The two began to laugh from deep down inside for several moments before they reached the gate that would allow them inside the wall. The guide opened it, and Dr. Marquez entered the banquet hall to the sound of laughter…beautiful, joyous, boisterous laughter.

www.ingramcontent.com/pod-product-compliance
Lightning Source LLC
Chambersburg PA
CBHW011031260626
47153CB00019B/2913